Bolan was dropping and spinning completely out of control

He felt adrenaline rush his system. He knew he was going to miss the road and be thrown into the dense copse of acacia trees beyond it.

He reached down and unsnapped the emergency release at his waist, letting his heavy pack fall away below him. The effect was immediately noticeable and his speed tempered, though he still rushed toward the trees at a deadly pace. Bolan reached up with both hands and clawed at the guides of his single inflated cell.

The Executioner bent himself almost double as he hauled on his lines, trying to twist his direction of fall away from the trees and back onto the road. For one wild second he thought he was going to make it, and his body swung in a compact turn.

Then his boots struck treetops and the final cell of the parachute collapsed.

MACK BOLAN ®
The Executioner

#275 Crossed Borders
#276 Leviathan
#277 Dirty Mission
#278 Triple Reverse
#279 Fire Wind
#280 Fear Rally
#281 Blood Stone
#282 Jungle Conflict
#283 Ring of Retaliation
#284 Devil's Army
#285 Final Strike
#286 Armageddon Exit
#287 Rogue Warrior
#288 Arctic Blast
#289 Vendetta Force
#290 Pursued
#291 Blood Trade
#292 Savage Game
#293 Death Merchants
#294 Scorpion Rising
#295 Hostile Alliance
#296 Nuclear Game
#297 Deadly Pursuit
#298 Final Play
#299 Dangerous Encounter
#300 Warrior's Requiem
#301 Blast Radius
#302 Shadow Search
#303 Sea of Terror
#304 Soviet Specter
#305 Point Position
#306 Mercy Mission
#307 Hard Pursuit
#308 Into the Fire
#309 Flames of Fury
#310 Killing Heat
#311 Night of the Knives
#312 Death Gamble
#313 Lockdown
#314 Lethal Payload
#315 Agent of Peril
#316 Poison Justice
#317 Hour of Judgment
#318 Code of Resistance
#319 Entry Point
#320 Exit Code
#321 Suicide Highway
#322 Time Bomb
#323 Soft Target
#324 Terminal Zone
#325 Edge of Hell
#326 Blood Tide
#327 Serpent's Lair
#328 Triangle of Terror
#329 Hostile Crossing
#330 Dual Action
#331 Assault Force
#332 Slaughter House
#333 Aftershock
#334 Jungle Justice
#335 Blood Vector
#336 Homeland Terror
#337 Tropic Blast
#338 Nuclear Reaction
#339 Deadly Contact
#340 Splinter Cell
#341 Rebel Force
#342 Double Play
#343 Border War
#344 Primal Law
#345 Orange Alert
#346 Vigilante Run
#347 Dragon's Den
#348 Carnage Code
#349 Firestorm
#350 Volatile Agent

The Executioner
Don Pendleton's ®
VOLATILE AGENT

A GOLD EAGLE BOOK FROM

W RLDWIDE ®

TORONTO • NEW YORK • LONDON
AMSTERDAM • PARIS • SYDNEY • HAMBURG
STOCKHOLM • ATHENS • TOKYO • MILAN
MADRID • WARSAW • BUDAPEST • AUCKLAND

First edition January 2008

ISBN-13: 978-0-373-64350-9
ISBN-10:   0-373-64350-0

Special thanks and acknowledgment to
Nathan Meyer for his contribution to this work.

VOLATILE AGENT

Printed in U.S.A.

He who seizes on the moment, he is the right man.
　　　　—Johann Wolfgang von Goethe 1749–1832

The moment I am called upon, I will not hesitate to do what needs to be done.
　　　　　　　　　　　　　　　　—Mack Bolan

THE
MACK BOLAN
LEGEND

Nothing less than a war could have fashioned the destiny of the man called Mack Bolan. Bolan earned the Executioner title in the jungle hell of Vietnam.

But this soldier also wore another name—Sergeant Mercy. He was so tagged because of the compassion he showed to wounded comrades-in-arms and Vietnamese civilians.

Mack Bolan's second tour of duty ended prematurely when he was given emergency leave to return home and bury his family, victims of the Mob. Then he declared a one-man war against the Mafia.

He confronted the Families head-on from coast to coast, and soon a hope of victory began to appear. But Bolan had broken society's every rule. That same society started gunning for this elusive warrior—to no avail.

So Bolan was offered amnesty to work within the system against terrorism. This time, as an employee of Uncle Sam, Bolan became Colonel John Phoenix. With a command center at Stony Man Farm in Virginia, he and his new allies—Able Team and Phoenix Force—waged relentless war on a new adversary: the KGB.

But when his one true love, April Rose, died at the hands of the Soviet terror machine, Bolan severed all ties with Establishment authority.

Now, after a lengthy lone-wolf struggle and much soul-searching, the Executioner has agreed to enter an "arm's-length" alliance with his government once more, reserving the right to pursue personal missions in his Everlasting War.

1

Mack Bolan reached under the dashboard of the Lincoln Navigator and worked the slide on the Beretta 93-R. The smooth action made a metallic snap as it maneuvered a 9 mm Parabellum round into the pistol chamber. The MX12 sound suppressor was a squat black cylinder on the end of the threaded muzzle. Bolan moved the fire-selector switch to the semiautomatic position and then slid the Beretta into place behind his back under his navy blue windbreaker.

Bolan sat up and looked through the tinted windows of the SUV, watching his prey nervously pacing in front of the men's bathroom in the city park. The man's name was Raphael Pucuro and he was a Confidential Informant for the DEA. Bolan narrowed his eyes and brought the man into focus, scanning the figure for every detail.

The park was almost deserted at the late hour. Halogen street lamps created halos of yellow light in staggered pools. Across the park a group of teenagers shouted and laughed as they played on the basketball courts. An elderly couple walked a black Labrador retriever along a paved path. On the far side of the recreation area several vehicles sat parked and silent, forming a wall between the grass and the street.

Pucuro was tall, as tall as Bolan, but whipcord thin with

the nervous habits and shaking hands of an addict. His hair was swept straight back from a pockmarked face. The CI had made a marginalized living working as a drug mule between Colombia and the United States, giving up tips on his competitors to stay out of prison.

Bolan considered what he knew about how Pucuro made the big time. As part of his dealings, he had been given a cell phone by his DEA handlers, one they were constantly locked into. He'd gotten lazy over the digital signal and sealed his fate. Pucuro had arranged for six ex-special operations soldiers working as security contractors to meet in Bogotá with members of Colombia's FARC terrorist group to arrange an information buy on behalf of American interests.

The meet had been a setup, and the Americans were machine-gunned in their car at a stoplight outside their hotel. DEA control had listened in as Pucuro had arranged payment. What they overheard had shocked them into alerting the Department of Homeland Security and from there Hal Brognola had quietly inserted himself into the situation.

In return for his help in setting up the private contractors Pucuro received a memory stick containing a communications list of all telephone numbers used by field administrators in the Directorate of Intelligence and Prevention Services for Venezuela. For strike two, instead of going to his DEA handlers, Pucuro tried to cut a deal with Chinese intelligence instead.

Brognola wanted the memory stick with those numbers, and the betrayed American operators cried out for justice. Bolan had been called in. If the CI wasn't willing to cooperate, he had sealed his own fate. The Executioner shadowed the man to the secluded park and was about to instigate an interception one step ahead of the Chinese retrieval team. Despite his crimes, Pucuro was a treasure vault of information and a live capture had been requested.

Bolan opened the door to the SUV and stepped out into the night. He wore blue jeans and hiking boots with his windbreaker. The dome light to the Navigator had been disabled, and he closed the door softly while Pucuro's back was turned. Bolan put his head down and shoved his hands into the pockets of his jacket as he set off across the grass.

The Executioner angled his approach across the corner of the athletic fields to keep the squat brick restroom building between himself and Pucuro. Bolan covered the ground quickly, looking casual but moving with purpose, like a man in a hurry to get to the bathroom. He reached the back wall of the structure and scanned the scene. On the street two men got out of a black sedan in the parking lot to his right. When he looked, Bolan saw nothing between himself and the basketball-playing teenagers on the left. He rounded the corner of the building.

Pucuro looked up, startled at Bolan's sudden appearance. His hand fell in a telltale sign toward the inside pocket of his thigh-length leather jacket. The big American held up his empty hands and smiled.

"Easy, friend," Bolan said in Spanish. "I just want to give you some money."

Pucuro's eyes flickered over Bolan's shoulder, and the Executioner knew the snitch was looking toward the two men approaching from the street. Pucuro looked back at Bolan. His hand darted back inside his jacket, and Bolan caught a glimpse of a nylon shoulder sling. The Executioner sprang into motion.

Bolan surged forward, sweeping up his left arm and catching the startled snitch high on his chest. His fist grasped Pucuro's jacket tightly while the elbow slammed into the other man's shoulder. Bolan drove the slighter man back behind the L-shaped concrete wall serving as a divider between public view and the open door to the men's bathroom.

"Don't be stupid," Bolan growled. "Let me help you come in."

Pucuro squawked in protest and stumbled back on his heels under Bolan's onslaught. His right hand emerged from his jacket around the butt of a black automatic pistol. Bolan's right hand emerged from his jacket pocket even as Pucuro's tried to claw his own weapon free. The Liquid Silver gravity knife opened as Bolan flicked his wrist.

The big American brought his arm up fast and hard, shoving the blade into Pucuro's solar plexus and penetrating the diaphragm. Pucuro gasped and air rushed from his lungs. Blood spilled out sticky and hot across Bolan's knuckles.

Bolan shoved Pucuro. The man bounced off the wall, and the soldier spun him into the open bathroom door. Pucuro's pistol, a compact Glock 19, hung loose in his hands. Bolan's fist lashed out again. The knife slid home under Pucuro's chin and more blood spilled, splattering the floor. The Glock dropped to the concrete with a clatter.

Bolan let the dead man fall, then dropped to one knee beside the corpse and began to frisk the body. He found a fat wallet inside one pocket. A business envelope tucked into Pucuro's other jacket pocket contained the memory stick.

Bolan carefully wiped the blade of his knife clean on the dead man's shirt. He rose to his feet and put the envelope in his own jacket pocket.

He heard footsteps on the concrete outside. They hit the ground rapidly, and Bolan knew whoever was approaching was doing so at a dead run. He spun and pulled the Beretta 93-R from behind his back.

The first of the two men Bolan had seen in the parking lot rounded the corner. He was dressed in a business suit and an overcoat. A flat, black automatic pistol filled his fist. Over the first man's shoulder the second man appeared, jockeying for position in the cramped quarters.

Bolan's gaze locked onto the Chinese agent's startled eyes. Both men raised their weapons. The big American threw himself to one side as he brought up the Beretta. The sound suppressor spit, and an instant later the tight chamber of the restroom reverberated with the sharp clap of a gunshot as the Chinese man fired simultaneously with an unmuffled pistol.

The Chinese agent staggered backward, a fount of blood opening up on his shoulder an inch above his heart. The man stumbled and his arms flew out as his pistol round rattled the metal divider around the toilets in the back of the room. Bolan bounced off the wall and spun, dropping to one knee.

Bolan pulled the trigger on his pistol again and buried a soft-nosed 9 mm round in the lead agent's forehead. The second man twisted at the waist, ducking out of the way of the tumbling body, and his own pistol came up around the falling corpse.

Bolan shot him through the heart.

The man's finger convulsed on his trigger, and the pistol bucked in his falling hand. A round flew past the crouching Bolan and shattered the thin, metal-backed glass of the restroom mirror. Splinters of glass showered the Executioner, sprinkling his hair and shoulders before falling to the floor.

The second agent hit the curve of the wall and slumped to the ground.

Bolan popped back up and quickly placed the still warm Beretta behind his back. He shook his head and ran a hand through his hair, spilling additional shards of glass onto the floor. He patted his pocket to make sure the memory stick was secure. Satisfied, he stood. Without hesitation he walked forward, stepped over the corpses and exited the restrooms.

The Executioner caught a glimpse of the teenagers across the park. They had stopped playing basketball and stood on the edge of the court, facing his direction. Several of them held up cell phones. He saw no sign of the elderly couple and their dog as he crossed the grass.

Moving quickly but staying calm, Bolan slid behind the wheel of the Lincoln Navigator. The big block engine purred to life immediately.

Bolan smoothly guided the big SUV out of the parking lot and into sparse traffic. He got out his cell phone and prepared to call Brognola. The big Fed had a mess that needed cleaning up.

2

The gunmen were in the hotel.

Crouched in the dark, Marie Saragossa eased the charging handle back on her mini-Uzi machine pistol. She chambered a 9 mm round and eased the receiver back into place. She pushed the safety selector onto the fire position. Out in the hallway beyond the door to her hotel room, Saragossa heard the murmur of deep male voices and the creaking of the floor under their footsteps.

Rain hammered the glass of the room's only window. Despite the downpour, the heat in the room was stifling. Saragossa wore an olive green tank top, and it stuck to her body like a second skin. Perspiration ran into the valley between her breasts, and she could feel beads of sweat slide across her abdomen and along the small of her back.

Saragossa clenched then relaxed her grip on the machine pistol. As a young girl in Castro's Cuba, she had been instructed in the use of weapons. Her subsequent rise into the intelligence service of the dictator's country had only sharpened those skills—skills she now sold on the open market in the true spirit of the capitalism she had been taught to hate as a child.

The men in the hallway fell silent. Saragossa looked over the bed she crouched behind. A satellite phone lay on top of the covers, her only link with the outside world. From the street she heard rough laughter over the falling rain, then the stuttering burst of a Kalashnikov. There was a scream followed by more laughter.

It wasn't supposed to be like this.

The rebels had driven across the border as night fell and had taken the town. The rains had rolled into the region, halting the government counteradvance in its tracks, and the rebels had begun an orgy of murder, torture, rape and looting. Intelligence indicated that the township of Yendere was a sanctuary point for the rebels and that they possessed a good relationship with the population on the Burkina Faso side of the border with the Ivory Coast.

Makimbo, Saragossa's last street contact in the township, told her all of that had changed when the rebel units found the drugs.

The border town of Yendere had become a transition point. The rebels had morphed, becoming a link in the narcotic routes from Latin America into Europe. Cocaine and heroin were introduced by ship into the Ivory Coast, then made their way by a variety of means across the border into Burkina Faso's capital of Ouagadougou. Only the rebel units who had arrived across the border one step ahead of Ivory Coast national forces hadn't been a part of the established network. When they found shipments of narcotics among the crates of sheep wool in the warehouses behind the township mosque, the frenzy had begun.

Now Makimbo was gone, along with every other person who could make their escape along the only road leading out of town. With her dusky skin and long, straight hair Saragossa had been trapped. Her principal had promised her help if she could hold out long enough, but that was a huge *if*.

The green light indicating battery charge on her sat phone glowed like a beacon in the dark room. Outside her door Saragossa heard whispers. Holding the machine pistol close to her face in her right hand, the woman reached across the bedspread and wrapped her fingers around the phone.

The doorknob rattled as a heavy hand fell across it. Saragossa drew the phone to her and turned off the power. The bed lay between her and the door. Already on her knees, she slowly lowered herself to her stomach behind the mattress and frame as the doorknob began to turn.

She had taken a gamble. If she had locked the door, then she would be announcing her presence to the rampaging troops. She had to simply hide until help arrived in the form of mercenaries, government troops or a moneyman. Saragossa had experienced many unpleasant things since her days as a girl in Cuba. Being raped was not one she wanted to endure ever again.

The door creaked loudly as the rebel outside pushed it open. Saragossa slid under the bed. Light from the hallway spilled into the room. From her position she saw a pair of bare, skinny ankles above a filthy pair of rubber-soled tennis shoes. The soles of the shoes were thick with mud, and the toes were splattered with dark splotches that could only be blood.

Saragossa eased her arm up from her side, bringing the mini-Uzi around should she need to use it. Her breathing sounded as loud as a furnace bellows to her. The rebel walked a few steps into the room. She smelled cheap tobacco burning and an almost overwhelming stench of body odor.

The material of Saragossa's shirt was stuck tight to the small of her back from the humidity and her own sweat. In the next moment she felt a fat weight drop onto her from the bottom of the mattress. She tensed in horror.

She felt the tiny presence scuttle up her back. She closed her eyes against the shudder of revulsion that threatened to ripple across her body. The thing was too short to be a centipede, but the legs felt too close together to be a spider. To Saragossa's mind that left two options—one creepy the other deadly. The first was a roach. West African roaches were prevalent, disgusting and huge. The second was a scorpion. If a Death Stalker scorpion was to crawl up her back and become entangled in the thick mass of her long hair, she knew she was in very real danger.

The poison of the Death Stalker was fierce, deadly in children and the elderly, and likely to make her so sick she'd be unable to save herself if the rebels attacked her. In the field pack hidden behind her under the bed she had a first-aid kit complete with antivenin shots for insects and snakes. But nothing would help her if she was discovered by the gunmen in the room.

The creature scurried up her body, and Saragossa bit down hard on her trembling lower lip to stifle any sound. A young bass voice called out something from the hallway. The thing perched between Saragossa's shoulder blades froze as the man in the room answered, his voice loud and slurred.

Saragossa held her breath. A sting from a scorpion that close to her spine and central nervous system could be fatal. If the gunmen discovered her under the bed and forced her to move and fire in self-defense, she was damned. There was no way that one of the aggressive African scorpion species would not strike.

Let it be a roach, she thought. Or a beetle. Let it be a goddamned dung beetle.

The man walked farther into the room. From where she lay Saragossa could see the ragged bottoms of the man's cutoff jeans hanging down past his knees. The gunman relaxed—apparently satisfied the room was empty—and lowered his weapon so that Saragossa could see the muzzle and front sight of the assault rifle.

She heard the light switch snap on and off and the man curse in frustration. She had unscrewed the lightbulbs earlier but left them in the outlet to make it appear as if they had only burned out. On her back the creature began to move again, climbing up her nape where her hair was held in place by a cloth strip from a field medic kit used to splint broken bones or wrap wounds.

A tiny puddle of sweat had pooled in the hollow there. She felt the hard, sticky legs of the creature play themselves across the goose bumps of her flesh as it paused, drinking in her perspiration. The monsoon rains had kept the malaria-bearing mosquitoes and potential deadly flies inactive, and Saragossa hadn't bothered using her insect repellant for days. She was an inviting playground to the bugs driven indoors by the rain.

The rebel opened the door to the hotel room all the way, spilling in more light. He dropped his half-smoked cigarette to the floor, and Saragossa watched him grind it out inches from her face. It lay on the room's only rug and smoldered. A trail of smoke streamed up from the half-crushed cigarette and into her face.

The weight at the back of her neck shifted with sudden purpose and scurried onto her left shoulder. She breathed out slowly and cautiously. Afraid to turn her head, Saragossa shifted her eyes to follow the gunman as he walked deeper into the room. Predictably, he was headed for the closet.

The legs on her shoulder began a lazy trail down her arm toward her elbow. The thing was in such disgustingly intimate contact with her that Saragossa was almost positive it was no cockroach or dung beetle.

The rebel opened the door to her closet and chuckled. He called out to the other gunman in the hallway, and then he started throwing Saragossa's luggage onto the bed. The mattress spring bounced in protest as her heavy backpack bounced onto the rickety bed.

The bed undulated above her, threatening to press down against her head. The thing on her arm froze in midstride. Saragossa could hear a hiss and knew without a doubt it was a scorpion. She felt a surge of adrenaline as her stomach clenched and sour bile flooded the back of her throat.

She heard footsteps and shifted her eyes to the door. The second gunman had entered to see what the first had found. This one wore dirty black sweatpants tucked into battered old army boots. He said something to the first gunman, and both pairs of feet crowded up to the bed.

Agitated, the scorpion crawled off Saragossa's arm, running down her bicep to the plank wood floor. She gritted her teeth against the horror of how close the thing was to her face, especially her eyes. She had felt the segmented serpentine sway of the arachnid's stinger as it slid off her arm.

Above her the bed bounced as the two gunmen began to open and rifle through her bags. Dust scattered by the activity trailed down into Saragossa's face. She shifted her eyes to the left, trying to see the scorpion, but her hair hung in her way.

Terrified, Saragossa risked moving her head. She felt the searching grasp of the creature's brittle-haired legs reach her left wrist. She felt the wiry folds of the front pincers bump across her skin as it climbed onto her hand.

She could see the thing clearly now. The arachnid had a brown banded back and abdomen set in the dull yellow amber color of the body. The stinger was raised like a fist over the segmented and armored torso. It was ugly and with a sinking sense of horrified certainty, Saragossa realized it was as deadly a scorpion as there was—the Death Stalker. Ounce for ounce it was one of the most poisonous creatures on the planet.

The rebels began to chatter in earnest. Articles of clothing began to litter the floor at their feet. A new voice called out from the hallway, and one of the men beside Saragossa's bed answered.

There was laughter from the hall, then the bed suddenly sagged as one of the rebels fell onto the mattress, roaring with laughter. The tired old bedsprings sang in protest, and the bottom sank so low it smacked Saragossa hard on the top of her head. Her chin bounced off the floor, and she hissed in surprise as she bit down on her tongue. The copper-tang metallic taste of blood filled her mouth. Her body tensed tight against the sudden pain.

That pain was nothing compared to what came next.

She felt like her hand had been struck by a baseball bat. She spasmed at the brutal, all encompassing shock of the scorpion strike. She bit down hard against the pain. Tears filled her eyes.

Then the scorpion struck again.

This time she couldn't control herself. The moan was ripped from her body. The scorpion scurried off her arm and disappeared into the gloomy shadows at the head of the bed. Through a prism of involuntary tears Saragossa's vision swam. She was in trouble.

The two men above her were quiet. For one long moment they were simply still and silent as the voice from the hallway called out to them. Then there was an explosion of motion.

The man on the bed sprang up and off the mattress, knocking Saragossa's luggage to the floor. The rebel gunman already standing ripped the cover of the bed up. Saragossa was suddenly confronted with a grimacing male face, eyes wide with emotion and red veined with drug use.

The man snarled something and a hand the size of a dinner plate reached out and grabbed her by the arm. Saragossa let herself be taken without a struggle.

Saragossa looked up as the gunman dragged her clear of the bed. The scorpion's poison was taking effect, and her vision had already begun to blur. Her left arm felt at once as if a hundred hot needles were gouging her, and as if it were made of lead.

She saw the gunmen looking down on her. Both men instinctively grabbed for the pistol grips of their Kalashnikovs, but at the sight of her small feminine form they relaxed and neither one assumed an aggressive stance with their assault rifles. Their bloodshot gazes roamed the curves of her body.

Saragossa whispered hate-filled curses at them in Spanish and brought up her mini-Uzi. Both men's eyes expanded in shock and dull-witted horror.

Saragossa was merciless.

She triggered the mini-Uzi, and the little kill box chattered and shook in her hand. She stitched a line of 9 mm slugs straight into the first man's throat. She shredded his neck, and the blood splattered across her upturned face even as the rebel was driven back. Hot shell casings bounced off the flat stretch of her belly.

Still firing, Saragossa shifted the compact machine pistol and took out the second man who stood frozen, mouth gaping. Her first two rounds hit his left deltoid and then shattered his collarbone before she put a bullet in his jaw, nasal cavity and right eye. The gunman crumpled without ever firing back.

Saragossa didn't think, didn't reflect, she merely acted. She pushed herself up to her knees and sprang to her feet. Her left arm hung useless from her side, as dead as the two African men lying on the floor behind her.

She crossed the room and was at the door while voices in the hallway were still calling out in confusion. She twisted around the door frame, her weapon already firing. The exertion made her dizzy, and her vision was badly blurred from the scorpion's neurotoxin. She caught the shape of a man, the hall light behind him, standing at the top of the stairs leading up from the front lobby.

She fired and knocked him down even as he triggered a burst of his own. The bullets from his assault rifle burrowed into the wall on her right, and Saragossa staggered off the door frame as he went down.

She rushed forward. There were blind spots in her eyes now, and she was frantic to kill all the rebels before she blacked out. She came to the top of the stairs and tripped over the outstretched arm of the man she had just killed. She fell hard and landed on her knees. A burst of automatic weapon fire passed through the space above her head.

Saragossa thrust out her arm and pointed the machine pistol down the narrow staircase. Her eyes were too dilated to focus, and she couldn't see much. She pulled the trigger and poured 9 mm rounds down the stairwell toward where she'd sensed the muzzle-flash.

She heard a cry. The man on the stairs gurgled loudly and dropped his weapon with a clatter onto the wooden steps. There was a sound like a basketball bouncing off a backboard as the rebel's head struck each step on his long slide down.

Saragossa fell backward.

She felt flushed all over and nauseous. She lurched to her feet and stumbled back toward the door to her room like a drunk.

She'd been stung twice, and she knew that was enough to kill her.

3

Bolan sat in the back of the plane. The five-seat Aérospatiale AS350 was a charter aircraft from West African Trans-Cargo—a front company used by American intelligence concerns operating out of Liberia. He sat with a pen and notepad, making a list of equipment he'd need for the operation while Barbara Price gave him operational details over a secured line and into the headset he wore.

"It's just you, Striker," Price said. "This intel came through last minute, and other Stony Man assets have already been committed globally."

"What's going on?"

"A convergence of events has given us a window of opportunity to exploit, and Washington wants to really push it. You were the quickest resource we could deploy on such short notice."

"This wet work?" Bolan asked.

"It could get pretty wet, but basically it's a snatch op."

"Who and why?"

"In the late eighties before Noriega was taken out, Langley was running an asset named Marie Saragossa inside the dictator's security service. After the regime fell she went free-lance. She's worked for just about everyone in the Southern Regional Operational Zone."

"Cartels? Castro?"

"Saragossa is mercenary. She doesn't take ideological sides, but she came out of Cuba. She worked for Castro, she worked for Pablo Escobar, but she also worked against them, for us. So Langley kept a loose leash on her to piggyback inside those camps."

"Did she know this?"

"Not always. Part of her contracts for us included payment in tech. Field gear and communications, mostly."

"So as payment she was given encoded sat phones, laptops, stuff like that. Equipment she'd never hope to score on the open market. Only we made sure we were keyed in," Bolan said.

"Exactly."

"Sounds familiar," Bolan said, his voice dry. "Go on."

"Last week Saragossa took a job for the president of Venezuela. A reconnaissance and procurement gig in Burkina Faso. Seems they got wind of some kind of operation that Hussein had going down before the Iraq war. So he made a play-for-pay deal and sent her to West Africa."

"With Langley watching every move?" Bolan asked.

"Exactly. With the information we got from Pucuro's memory stick we could monitor almost all aspects of this event from all the players, not just Saragossa. Only as insane as South American politics can get, West Africa's got 'em beat hands down. Whatever Saragossa was looking for, it was in the west of the country, along the border with the Ivory Coast."

"I'm not up on that region," Bolan admitted. "Are Ivory Coast and Burkina Faso engaged in hostilities?"

"Not openly, but the situation just went to hell. Both countries are controlled by military strongmen accused of corrupting elections to stay in power. They have a dispute about a couple of border markers. The Ivory Coast is in the middle of a three-way civil war. To give themselves some leeway Burkina Faso has been allowing members of the MPCI, the Ivory Coast Patriotic Movement, to use the area as a cross-border sanctuary."

"So what happened?"

"Whatever Saragossa was looking for, she discovered its location," Price said. "Unfortunately for her, two days ago the Ivory Coast national army began an offensive against the MPCI forces. They pushed them back across the border with Burkina Faso and kept on pushing right into the southern part of that country. The entire region is a combat zone with MPCI guerrilla units battling Ivory Coast government troops. Burkina Faso is massing its forces in the area, and if African Union diplomatic negotiators don't reach a compromise quickly, we're looking at another cross-border bush war."

"Saragossa is caught in the middle of this?" Bolan asked.

"Yesterday Langley's signal op center for this region intercepted a sat phone call by Saragossa to her Venezuelan control. Her township, Yendere, was overrun by elements of the MPCI who are now surrounded by army units. She's trapped in a hotel in the center of town and under fire."

"So I ride in on a white horse and she's so grateful she gives us Saddam's secrets?"

"It's not quite that simple, I'm afraid. Venezuela really wants what Saragossa has. Plus, some intercepts suggest that Saragossa may have used her feminine charms on the president and he's got a personal stake in her getting home."

"Does Venezuela have the resources to pull a rescue operation off in western Africa?" Bolan asked.

"No. But they do have billions in oil money now that he's nationalized all the wells in Venezuela. So he reached out to one James du Toit, former South African Defense Force special operator turned mercenary."

"I've heard that name. Wasn't du Toit mixed up in some bad business in New Guinea a while back?"

"Correct. He just got out of prison in New Guinea for his role in the failed coup attempt there. He's got aircraft, soldiers and a logistics network throughout the continent. Venezuela has the cash, du Toit has the capabilities. From what Venezuelan intelligence told Saragossa, du Toit's deploying a platoon in a Super Puma helicopter to pull her out of the firefight."

"So she's not going to be all that happy to see me," Bolan stated.

"No. You have to get in ahead of the South Africans, convince Saragossa by any means necessary to flip, and then extract her from the middle of the Yendere township, which is currently filled with MPCI guerrilla gunmen and surrounded by hostile army troops from the Ivory Coast."

"With Burkina Faso forces closing in," Bolan added.

"That's right," Price agreed.

Bolan fitted the drum magazine into a Mk 48 light weight machine gun. The weapon's green plastic drum snapped into place with a reassuring click. Bolan took the loose belt of 7.62 mm ammunition and fit it into place before slapping the feed tray cover down and locking it into place.

"All right. Let's talk details," he said after thinking things over.

Price immediately began filling Bolan in on the logistical and support elements of the last minute, rapid deployment operation.

4

Saragossa lunged for her pack. Her left hand was frozen, cramped, and she worked at the buckles and drawstring with only her right. She felt her throat squeezing closed, and forced air into her lungs with a harsh, wheezing sound. She managed to open the first-aid pack, then bent down, using her teeth to help prise off the Velcro fastener on the top flap pouch.

Her all-purpose antivenin kit spilled out. Her throat closed up and she made a high-pitched barking sound like a seal, a condition known as stridor. Two breaths later Saragossa realized air was no longer making it through. Her mind was a white blank of panic. Death hugged her close. She opened the kit, but her shaking hand spilled the contents across her lap.

Her heart lurched abruptly in her chest. She knew she was dying. She didn't know what to do. She didn't know whether to use the venom-antagonist to neutralize the poison or to use shock medicine syringes. She fumbled ineffectually as her vision continued to dim around the edges.

Saragossa looked down. Her lap felt as if it were a mile away. She lifted her arm, and the feeling was completely disassociated. It could have been someone else's arm for all she felt connected to it. She felt for the epi-pen and thumbed off the cap. It was military-grade atropine meant to counter chemical or biological warfare agents in addition to more pedestrian utilizations.

She lifted her arm as her vision went completely black, though her eyes remained open. She felt a falling sensation and snapped her arm down. The spring-loaded syringe shot into her leg and the needle discharged. She was immediately jolted back into herself. The effect on her airway was nearly instant.

She dropped the autoinjector and sucked in a lungful of life-giving air. She could breathe, but the adrenaline-hormone cocktail only added to the feeling of crushing pressure in her chest. She scooped up her kit and plucked out a little brown bottle. She put her teeth against the snap lid and let two tiny white pills fall out into her mouth.

She caught the nitroglycerin pills under her tongue and let them dissolve there. The pressure in her chest began to ease. She dropped the bottle and reached for her antivenin kit. She felt much better, but knew she was still in dire trouble. So far she was only combating symptoms and side effects— deadly symptoms and side effects, but still only secondary presentations.

She saw the green autoinjector filled with venom-antagonist. She juggled the syringe with fingers that felt as thick as sausage links. She pushed the nose of the autoinjector pen against her hand in the meaty part beneath the thumb.

The infected hand still burned, and the needle felt icy cold as it punched into the venom-filled muscle. Saragossa dropped the injector and sagged back against the wall, fighting for air and terrified by the continued crushing pressure behind her sternum.

The tablets continued dissolving beneath her tongue as she lay there, helpless. Breathe, she told herself, just breathe.

She lay helpless in the stink, the heat and the damp, and concentrated on breathing in and out. She thought about nothing else beyond filling her lungs with good air, then pushing out the bad air.

Gradually she felt the pressure reduce to a simple feeling of heaviness. Then, as the muscles of her abdomen began to unknot, that too dissipated. She was covered in sweat. She lay with her head on the ground and lifted her feet up and rested them on her pack. She knew by elevating her extremities she reduced the workload of her heart.

Saragossa pulled her machine pistol closer to her. She rested for a moment after the activity and let her breathing even out and her heart rate slow. When she felt stronger, she reached over and grabbed her left wrist with her right hand and rested it across her chest. She paused to take in her surroundings. She could detect no immediate threats and focused on taking care of herself.

She looked at the scorpion stings. Her veins stood out in vivid relief, and red streaks turned her dusky colored skin ashen from the puncture wounds in her hand. Pustules were already forming into fat pimples above the sting marks. In a few minutes she would need to pop and drain them before covering the area with antibiotic ointment and a clean, dry dressing.

In this kind of an environment infection would set in quickly and hang on stubbornly. Saragossa knew her arm, despite the work of the venom-antagonist in killing the active poison, was damaged by the necrotic effects of the scorpion stings and would continue to be hampered until a full recovery was made.

But she didn't have time for a full recovery. She had a tight schedule for operations. She needed the use of her arm immediately. Saragossa scooted over to one side. Now that she was breathing freely she reached into her pack and pulled her general first-aid bag free.

Moving slowly and becoming more clearheaded by the moment, Saragossa opened the minipack and began to rummage through her kit. She pulled out two syringe bundles held together by white medical tape. Pulling her boot knife free, she slipped the tip of the blade under the tape and in between two of the syringes before plucking a single needle free.

Saragossa took the syringe filled with antinausea medicine and pulled the needle cover off with her teeth. She spit the plastic cap away and stuck the needle into her exposed shoulder. She pushed the plunger down and injected the medicine smoothly before discarding the syringe, needle down, into the wooden plank of the floor.

The next bundle she opened was a painkiller. The narcotic would completely numb the area it was injected into. It had euphoric side effects that Saragossa knew could hamper her judgment, but without it her left arm would be useless. After injecting her shoulder she repeated the process in the exposed muscles of her inflamed forearm.

Saragossa tossed the needle aside and picked up the feeder tube from the water bladder in her pack. She sucked slowly, drinking carefully. Then she lay still for twenty minutes, collecting herself.

As she let her medical cocktail take effect, Saragossa began the process of survival. Carefully she began to compartmentalize the incident, to wall it off away from the front of her mind. It was just something that had happened.

"Bad day, screw it," she whispered.

She pushed the fear away, along with the helpless rage and the queasy sensation that the memory of the scorpion clutching tightly with its prickly legs to her hand gave her. She pushed the memories and the feelings down, then bricked them over. She began to test her senses, taking in stimulation from the building around her. She heard a scream over the drone of falling rain.

She slid her boot knife away and slowly secured the loose parts of her medical supplies before packing them back into the first-aid bag and the smaller antivenin kit. After glancing at her hand Saragossa slid the antivenin kit into the cargo pocket on her leg instead of putting it back in the top of the backpack.

She slowly rose into a sitting position. The feeling of dizziness nearly caused her to swoon, but the sensation passed. She lifted her red and swollen arm and looked at it. She felt no pain. She experimented with opening and closing her hand. The motion was stiff but didn't hurt. She looked at her watch and frowned.

It was then that a multitude of weapons opened fire on her room.

5

Bolan shoved a fistful of local currency over the battered seat to the cabdriver and got out. He leaned in the open window of the passenger door and instructed the driver to wait for him around the block. The taxi sped away, leaving him standing on the edge of an unpaved street. There was an open sewer off to his right, and the stench was ripe in his nose.

The Executioner looked around. He was on the opposite side of the township of Banfora from the international airport. Banfora was the capital of Komoe, Burkina Faso's southwesternmost province and the one sharing a border with Ivory Coast. The dirt street was lined with shanties, and what light there was escaped from boarded-up windows or from beneath shut doors. A pair of mongrels fought over some scraps in a refuse pile several yards up the road. Other than those dogs fighting, the stretch of grimy road was deserted.

The previous day, intelligence had noted that a brigade-sized element complete with field artillery and armored vehicles had been speeding through the regional center toward the villages of the border area. War had come once again to one of the poorest countries in the world.

Faintly, Bolan could hear the sound of music playing and then voices raised in argument. A baby started crying somewhere, and farther away more dogs began barking in response. Bolan looked up at the sky, noting the low cloud cover. The road was thick with muck from the seasonal rains, and it clung to the soles of his hiking boots.

Bolan set down the attaché case he was holding and reached around behind his back to pull his pistol clear. He jacked the slide and chambered a .44 Magnum round before sliding it into his jeans behind his belt buckle, leaving it in plain sight. He leaned down and picked up the case. He shifted his grip on the handle so that his gun hand was free.

Bolan took a quick look around before crossing the road and stepping up to the front door of one of the innumerable shacks lining the road. He lifted his big hand and pounded three times on the door. He heard a hushed conversation break out momentarily before the voices fell quiet.

"Le Crème?" Bolan asked.

Bolan felt a sudden damp and realized it had started to rain while he was standing there. Despite the wet, he was still uncomfortably warm in his short-sleeve, button-down khaki shirt and battered blue jeans.

The door opened slowly and a bar of soft light spilled out and illuminated him. A silhouette stood in the doorway, and Bolan narrowed his eyes to take in the figure's features. It was a male, wearing an unbuttoned and disheveled gendarme uniform.

He held a bottle of grain alcohol in one hand, and the other rested on the pistol grip of a French MAT-49 submachine gun hanging from a strap slung across his neck like a guitar. He leaned forward, crowding Bolan's space. The big American made no move to back up.

"Cooper?" the man asked.

His breath reeked with alcohol fumes, and the light around him reflected wildly off the glaze in his eyes. His words were softly slurred, but his gaze was steady as he eyed Bolan up and down. The finger on the trigger of the MAT-49 seemed firm enough.

"Yes." Bolan repeated. "Is Le Crème here?"

"Colonel Le Crème," the man corrected.

"Is *Colonel* Le Crème here?"

"You have the money?"

Bolan lifted the attaché case, though he knew the man had already seen it when he'd opened the door. The gendarme ignored the displayed satchel, his eyes never leaving Bolan's face. His hair was closely cropped, and Bolan could see bullets of sweat beading on the man's forehead.

"Give me the pistol," the man ordered.

"Go to hell," Bolan replied.

The drunken gendarme's eyes widened in shock and his face twisted in sudden, instant outrage. He snapped straight up and twisted the MAT-49 around on its sling, trying to bring the muzzle up in the cramped quarters.

Bolan's free hand shot out and grabbed the submachine gun behind its front sight. He locked his arm and pushed down, preventing the gendarme from raising the weapon. The gendarme's eyeballs bulged in anger, and the cords of his neck stood out as he strained to bring the submachine gun to bear.

"Leave him!" A deep bass voice barked from somewhere behind the struggling gendarme.

The man cursed and tried to step back and swing his weapon up and away from Bolan's grip. The Executioner stepped forward as the man stepped back, preventing the smaller man from bringing any leverage to bear.

They moved into the room, and Bolan heard chair legs scrape against floorboards as men jumped to their feet. He ignored them, making no move for the butt of the Desert Eagle sticking out of his jeans.

The man grunted his exertion and tried to step to the outside. Bolan danced with him, keeping the gendarme's body between him and the others in the smoky room. Bolan's grip on the front sling swivel remained unbroken. Finally, the gendarme dropped his bottle and grabbed the submachine gun with both his hands. The bottle thumped loudly as it struck the floor but did not break. Liquid began to gurgle out and stain the floorboards.

"I said enough!" the voice roared.

The gendarme was already using both his hands to snatch the submachine gun free as the order came. Bolan released the front sling swivel and stepped to the side. The gendarme found his center of balance around the struggle abruptly gone and overextended himself. Already drunk, he toppled backward and struck the floor in the pool of alcohol spilling from his fallen bottle.

Cursing and sputtering, the man tried to rise. Bolan surveyed the room. He saw four other men in the same soiled and rumpled police uniforms, each one armed either with a pistol or a submachine gun. All of them were gaunt and lanky with short hair, except for the bear of a man with the gold braid epaulets of an officer.

The officer rose from behind a table and hurled a heavy glass tumbler at the gendarme Bolan had left on the floor. The glass struck the man in the face and opened a gash under his eye.

"I said leave him!"

The shock of being struck snapped the embarrassed man out of his rage. He touched a hand to the cut under his eye and held up his bloody fingers. He looked away from his hand and nodded once toward the man looming behind the table.

The officer turned toward Bolan. "My apologizes," he said. "My men worry about my safety."

"Understandable, Colonel Le Crème." Bolan nodded. "I worry about my own safety."

"Come now, you are in the company of police officers."

"Yes, I am," Bolan agreed.

"Foreigners are not usually permitted to carry weapons in our land."

Bolan threw the attaché case on the table. "That should more than cover any administrative fees."

"Is it in euros?"

"As you specified."

Le Crème nodded, and one of the gendarmes at the table reached over and picked up the case. He had a sergeant's chevrons on his sleeve. Bolan saw there were two very young girls pressed up against the back wall of the shack. Their eyes were as hard as diamonds and glittered as they took him in.

The sergeant pulled the case over and opened it. The sudden light of avarice flared in his eyes, impossible to disguise. Bolan shrugged it off. He was tempted to believe that if he'd been born into the kind of poverty these men took for granted he might have been just as greedy.

While the sergeant counted the stacks of bills, the colonel reseated himself. He snapped his fingers at one of the girls, and she jumped to pick a fresh glass off a shelf beside her. She brought it over to the table and poured the colonel a drink from an already open bottle. Bolan could feel the intensity of her gaze.

Le Crème regarded Bolan through squinty, bloodshot eyes. He picked a smoldering cigar off the table and drew heavily from it. His men made no move to return to their seats. Le Crème pulled his cigar out of his mouth and gestured with it.

"Sit down."

Bolan pulled out the chair opposite Le Crème and eased

himself into it. The two men regarded each other with coolly assessing gazes while the sergeant beside Le Crème continued counting the money. Le Crème lifted his new glass and downed its contents without changing expression.

"Shouldn't a man like you be out hunting terrorists?" Le Crème asked.

"Shouldn't you be down in Banfora with the fighting?" Bolan asked.

Le Crème shrugged. "That's what the army is for. I fight crime."

"Just so."

The sergeant looked up from the money. Le Crème's eyes never left Bolan. "Is it all there?" he asked.

"More," the sergeant replied.

"Why?" Le Crème asked Bolan.

"There's a bonus in there. The shipment came in at a few more kilos than we'd originally talked about."

"Still tractor parts?"

"Yes."

"Okay then, no problem. It's St. Pierre's day on the Customs Desk," Colonel Le Crème said, smirking.

Bolan followed the line of Le Crème's sight across the room to where the gendarme Bolan had scuffled with stood glowering.

"Any way you want it, Colonel," Bolan said.

"Yes. Yes, it usually is."

Le Crème leaned back from the table and stretched out his arm. The girl who'd poured his drink slid into his lap. She regarded Bolan from beneath hooded lids. He guessed she could have been no older than sixteen. She was beautiful, her eyes so darkly brown they were almost black, but still nearly luminescent. The effect was disquieting. In America she would be in high school. In Burkina Faso she was the paramour of a corrupt warlord three times her age.

Bolan forced himself to look away.

The sergeant on Le Crème's right shut the briefcase and placed it on the floor at his colonel's feet. Bolan looked around the room. An expensive-looking portable stereo played hip-hop music featuring a French rapper. A bar stood against one wall and a motley collection of bottles sat on it, devoid of import tax stamps. Cigar smoke was thick in the room.

Bolan placed his hands palm down on the table and pushed himself up. He rose slowly and nodded to the colonel, who didn't bother to return the favor. Bolan looked over at the gendarme who had opened the door. The man's eyes were slits of hate.

The big American crossed the room, keenly aware of how many guns were at his back. He placed his hand on the door and slowly turned the knob. Coolly he swung it open and stepped out into the falling rain.

As he pulled the door closed behind him, Bolan saw headlights coming down the road. He stepped into the shadows beside the door and let his hand rest on the butt of the Desert Eagle. He didn't want to offer too great a silhouette in case this was some kind of hit squad, nor was he eager to be splashed by any of the offal in the ditches lining the road.

The headlights slowed and finally the car stopped directly in front of Bolan. He saw it was a taxi, not unlike the one he had waiting for him around the corner. The back door opened and a big man climbed out. He was Caucasian, and as he climbed out his windbreaker swung open. Bolan saw two pistols tucked into twin shoulder holsters.

Bolan let his hand fall away from the butt of his pistol and assumed a neutral stance. The man rose to his full height and

turned toward Bolan. He was square jawed and wide shouldered, his hair and beard both full and reddish tinged. When
he faced the Executioner they stood eye to eye.

A scar turned the corner of the man's mouth up in a per-
petual sneer, and his skin was ruddy and heavily pockmarked
over strong, almost bluntly Germanic features. He was holding a battered leather briefcase in one big hand. A gold signet
ring sat on one thick pinkie.

Bolan nodded. The man sized him up like a professional
boxer and then, almost grudgingly, nodded back. The man obviously knew why Bolan, a Westerner, was there. It was the
same reason the man himself had come to this place.

Bolan turned and began walking down the street toward
where he had instructed his own taxi to wait for him. Behind
him Bolan heard the man knock on the same door he himself
had, just minutes before. A voice answered from inside, and
the man said something in a crude French patois. His accent
was unmistakably Afrikaans.

As soon as he heard the voice any doubt Bolan might have
held was gone. That was the man he had been sent to stop.

6

After the initial burst of automatic weapons fire riddled the wall outside the window to her room, the firing simply stopped. Remaining in a low profile, Saragossa waited out a tense fifteen minutes.

She heard movement in the street and she went carefully over to the shot out window. In the street below she saw armed men running through the square. The motley crew of brigands ran in and out of the UNICEF offices and the front gate of the mudbrick wall surrounding the main Yendere mosque. Islam was by no means the dominant religion in Burkina Faso, but the mosques were almost always the most dominant buildings in any given town in the country.

Weak, Saragossa leaned back against the wall of her room. She thought about making for the roof and decided against it. From the lobby below her she could hear men calling back and forth to each other in rough voices.

She felt flushed with fever, and perspiration dripped off her in sheets. She hurt all over, and she knew she had been irrevocably slowed down. She was no longer confident in her ability to hold out if she had to fend off another attack. She hadn't packed enough ammunition to recreate the Bay of Pigs. The entire Burkina operation had been planned for one hell of a lot lower profile than it had turned out to be.

Saragossa went over to the bed and searched among her gear until she found her cell phone. She knew better than to think she'd get a signal, but the battery was fresh and other usage options on the device worked.

She crossed to the dresser and pulled out of the top drawer the legal tablet she used for her notes. On the first page, written in her tight, neat hand, was a summary of the information she had gathered about the Iraqi laboratory. This included a brief physical description of the building, its architecture and structural capabilities, a ten-digit grid coordinate and a precise GPS listing, as well as concise notes on the surrounding topography. It was everything she had been paid to deliver stripped down to the bare bone essentials. Using those notes, her intention had been to type up a full report for delivery to the principal in Caracas.

If push came to shove, however, everything they needed, all the information they had paid for, was on that sheet of paper. Saragossa settled herself back down below the window. The rain coming in through the shattered pane felt good against her feverish skin. With her back to the wall she could cover the door, and she kept her mini-Uzi close.

She placed the legal pad between her legs and opened her cell phone. She quickly tapped through her menu and selected the camera option. Carefully she centered the lens on the page. She drew the camera back, bringing the words on the paper into sharp focus. She held her hand steady and clicked the picture.

When that was done, she shut the phone and tore off the sheet with her notes on it, separating it from the legal pad. She folded the paper into quarters, then began ripping them into tiny pieces. When she was done she made a pile on the floor between her legs and used a match from her medic kit to light them.

The paper was consumed in seconds.

Still nauseous Saragossa leaned her head back against the wall. She cradled the mini-Uzi and prayed for her rescue to arrive.

7

Bolan walked into the airport terminal out of the rain. He wore a dark, hooded poncho, and water ran off him in erratic rivers. He scanned the waiting area of the open room and saw the gendarme from the previous night lounging against the wall by a folding table set in front of the small side room that was the customs station. Three other gendarmes and two men in army uniforms were scattered around the nearly deserted room.

The Banfora airport was an international operation. Burkina Faso was so small that it was possible to reach a host of other countries from any of the country's thirty-three airports, only two of which boasted paved runways. Because of this even the smallest of air terminals held a gendarme contingent for customs administration and at least a small force for security against insurrection. From the looks of the nearly empty terminal, it appeared that almost the entirety of the army had been moved toward the border with Ivory Coast to meet the incursion there.

The gendarme turned toward Bolan as soon as he saw him. Bolan pulled a manila envelope out from under his poncho as the man began walking toward him. The big American tossed the thick envelope onto one of the seats in a row of hard plastic chairs. He saw the man's eyes follow the envelope. When he looked up at Bolan again, the Executioner tapped

the face of his watch meaningfully, then turned and walked
back out into the rain.

Bolan walked around the edge of the terminal and crossed
a muddy stretch of grass before walking into the tall grass bor-
dering the airport. The land was mostly undulating plains
filled with tall grass and short, brushlike trees. Bolan knew
as he moved closer to the border the terrain would become
increasingly hilly.

Setting up behind a stand of short acacia trees, Bolan
watched the area through a pair of binoculars. After several
minutes he saw a soldier leave the terminal and run over to a
vehicle parked beside a rusting hangar. The soldier started up
an old truck with a canvas-covered bed and drove to the front
of the airport terminal. As soon as the truck pulled to a stop,
Le Crème's gendarme strolled out of the building and climbed
up into the cab beside the driver.

Behind him the rest of the security unit followed, clamber-
ing over the tailgate and into the back of the truck. As soon
as the last man was in, those in the back shouted something
and the truck pulled away from the terminal and drove down
the access road toward the highway leading into the township.

Bolan watched them go, satisfied for the moment. The operation had been so rushed there had been no time to imple-
ment a more comprehensive strategy than the one just
executed. When Bolan was finished, it would take even more
cash at even higher levels of government to smooth the
incident over. What Le Crème thought was a smuggling operation was something very different.

Briefly, Bolan considered moving his operations into one
of the hangars or even inside the terminal itself. It mattered
little if the few remaining civilian officials saw his face. But
he dismissed the idea. If everything didn't unfold precisely,

he wanted as little potential for collateral damage as possible. In a country where the life expectancy was barely fifty years of age, the people didn't need to be shot for political machinations for which they weren't responsible.

Bolan looked at his watch. Communication with Stony Man pilot Jack Grimaldi was based on an arranged timetable. Grimaldi would begin his approach in the Cessna Conquest I in ten minutes. Once he landed the pilot would turn the airplane and point the nose straight back up one leg of the twin strips with engines idling, prepared for an immediate takeoff.

Bolan caught a flash of movement and turned. A Land Rover pulled off the highway and began to speed down the terminal access road. Bolan zeroed in the binoculars on the vehicle windshield. James du Toit's square head came into focus behind the wheel. Bolan felt a grim satisfaction. Du Toit appeared to be grinning madly at some private joke. His lips moved as he said something to someone else in the vehicle.

Bolan frowned and refocused the binoculars. He zoomed in on the South African mercenary again.

Suddenly a pile of black hair rose from du Toit's lap, standing between him and the steering wheel. Bolan cursed in frustration. The girl from Le Crème's shack snuggled into the comfortable passenger seat of the vehicle. The Land Rover pulled up to the airport terminal. Bolan ground his teeth together in frustration.

He didn't know why the girl was there. Maybe du Toit had given Le Crème such a generous payoff the corrupt gendarme colonel had simply thrown the girl in as a bonus. Maybe du Toit had just bought her. Hell, Bolan thought, maybe she was the guy's wife, the *why* didn't really matter at the moment.

The steady drizzle of rain began to increase. The stiff breeze shifted slightly, and the orange wind sock on top of the terminal spun in a different direction. Bolan watched as the pair got out of the Land Rover and entered the terminal. He had just minutes to figure out how to change his plans.

She's not important, Bolan tried to tell himself. He didn't like how it sounded, even in his head. She had chosen her company, and he couldn't be held responsible for that. His life and the life of Marie Saragossa were on the line. Bolan frowned. He knew what he was getting into, had always known, and it had been his choice. Saragossa was a mercenary at heart. She'd turned down a hundred opportunities to get out of the game since Noriega had fallen. She was in Burkina Faso by choice.

Bolan knew it would be easy for him to extrapolate how many lives could depend on the information that Marie Saragossa held, but it didn't feel right in the face of a girl cursed by poverty to a short, brutal life. He couldn't kill her. She was, when all was said and done, an innocent.

Bolan looked at his watch, then back up to the sky. Right on time Bolan's sensitive ears picked up the sounds of the Cessna Conquest's big, prop-driven engine. Grimaldi was approaching for his landing. Bolan reached for his sat phone, prepared to scrub the mission. His eyes fell across his little cache. He saw the clackers for the Claymore mines he had set out along the runway where the helipad was located. It was more than enough to take out a Super Puma as it landed, destroying du Toit's transportation and putting down his eighteen-man strike force.

Claymores were indiscriminate killers, and the back blast area was significant. If du Toit pulled the Land Rover up next to the helipad to rendezvous with his team, the girl would be gravely injured. At best.

Grimaldi landed the plane smoothly despite the heavy rain

and crosswind. He began to brake the aircraft as he guided it toward the terminal. Its rear end skidded out to the side slightly as the rear landing gear slid in the mud on the runway. On board the plane the rest of Bolan's equipment for the mission was secured. Bolan knew he needed his long weapons. While he had wreaked considerable havoc before through the use of his Beretta and the Desert Eagle, he was going into a war zone when he left Banfora. It would be suicide to consider completing the operation armed as he was.

Bolan, his mind racing, debated with himself as Grimaldi taxied the plane into position. At that moment, from over Bolan's shoulder, came the rhythmic thumping of a powerful helicopter engine. Du Toit had managed to place his troops and equipment in the area of operations in just hours despite the heavy rains.

Bolan watched the terminal, hoping du Toit would leave the girl in the building when he came out to meet his men.

Grimaldi reached the end of the runway and turned the plane smoothly, his tires leaving deep ruts in the muddy strip as he did so. From above Bolan's head the racket of the helicopter coming in obscured all other sounds. A doorway set next to the observation window opened and du Toit walked out, heading toward the helicopter pad.

Bolan gripped the binoculars. Stay inside, he silently willed the girl. But she emerged from the terminal right behind du Toit.

The pair approached the landing pad as the helicopter hovered into position and the pilot began to lower the powerful aircraft. Bolan had placed his mines on either side of the pad, away from the raised dirt mound, camouflaging them and the detonation cord carefully so they were positioned in a V-pattern facing out from the rear of the helipad.

Bolan watched du Toit and the girl standing on the edge of the landing pad. The South African gave the pilot a thumbs-up as the skids touched down on the muddy soil. Bolan made up his mind. He was willing to risk detonating the Claymore on the far side.

He reached over and pulled the detonation clacker to him. He covered the edge and double-checked the electrical connection by looking for the blinking light in the small, recessed window of the detonator. The connection was good. Bolan looked up.

The pilot began to power down the rotors. Du Toit stepped away from the girl and approached the crew doors as they slid open on either side of the helicopter cargo bay. Beyond the helicopter landing pad Bolan saw the door set inside the frame of the Cessna open up and Grimaldi kick a short rope ladder out the side.

Bolan set his jaw hard and squeezed the detonation clacker.

The Claymores positioned on the far side of the helicopter erupted. Shrapnel slammed into the side of the Super Puma with ruthless efficiency. The frame of the aircraft shrieked in protest, and flight-tempered glass shattered. The explosion was murderously loud, but Bolan could hear the mercenaries' screams immediately.

Metal struts positioned at the point where the main rotor shaft met the roof of the helicopter shredded under the impact of the steel ball bearings, and the still spinning blades drooped dangerously. Bolan realized that if he triggered the second Claymore the mortality rate would be final for the South African mercenaries. He looked at the girl, hating that she was there, but he couldn't bring himself to do the smart thing.

Du Toit had been thrown to the ground and behind him the girl cowered at the explosion. Du Toit rose and pulled the pistols under his arms clear of their nylon holsters. Wounded mercenaries stumbled out of the helicopter, holding injuries, their clothes soaked in blood.

Bolan came up with the Beretta 93-R ready. He thumbed the selector switch to the triburst setting and hooked the thumb of his free hand through the oversized trigger guard. He swiveled, running for the terminal from his concealed position.

Du Toit saw the motion and spun, his pistols coming up. Even across the distance Bolan could see the other man's eyes widen in the shock of recognition. The Afrikaner's face hardened in determination, and he triggered the twin pistols.

Bolan fired the Beretta twice, aiming low and letting the recoil climb the muzzle up as six rounds spit out, speeding toward du Toit. Bolan's rounds flew wide as du Toit's own shots tore into the turf two steps behind the Executioner. With each stride Bolan's feet jarred into the mud and falling rain slashed at his face, forcing him to squint against its force.

Behind du Toit, Bolan saw the scrambling mercenaries heading for cover, some helping their wounded comrades, others simply throwing themselves into mud puddles in an effort to escape the flying lead. Bolan triggered two more bursts, but du Toit was already scrambling and the falling rain obscured the Executioner's aim.

Bolan reached the corner of the terminal and raced around it. Mud splashed up his pant legs as he ran along the front of the building. Through the windows he saw the few remaining civilians, clerks and customers, rushing toward the back observation window that opened out to the landing strips.

Out of sight of du Toit, Bolan continued sprinting down the length of the terminal. He came up to du Toit's Land Rover and pumped two bursts into the vehicle, puncturing the radiator and front passenger-side tire. Bolan risked a glance behind him as he neared the rear of the vehicle.

Du Toit came around the corner low, his pistols leading the way. Bolan twisted into a side shuffling gait and lowered the Beretta to his waist before triggering a quick blast at the crouching mercenary. The shots scored the side of the building, knocking chips of masonry flying and forcing du Toit to duck back around the sharp corner.

Bolan scurried behind the back of the Land Rover and went to one knee. Filthy water soaked the material of his jeans, chilling him unexpectedly. He took the Beretta into two hands and drew a bead on the edge of the terminal.

Du Toit did a quick sneak and peek around the edge of the building after changing his elevation in an attempt to try to throw off Bolan's aim. A gust of wind blew stinging drops of rain into the big American's face. He triggered the Beretta, missing du Toit but forcing him to duck back around the building edge once again.

Bolan popped to his feet, weapon held in front of him, and shuffled toward the corner of the building opposite du Toit. He fired the Beretta tight against the line of the terminal front wall to keep du Toit's head down, then turned and sprinted the last few yards for the edge of the building.

Twisting in midstride, Bolan muscled himself around the corner of the terminal. He put his head down and ran for the tail of the Cessna even as he heard Grimaldi revving the engines to a feverish pitch of mechanical intensity. Bolan hit the danger area between the cover of the building and the safety of the airplane at a dead sprint. He pumped his arms and raced flat out toward Grimaldi's aircraft.

Bolan risked a look over his shoulder as he ran and saw confused mercenaries fanning out for cover on the edge of the airport landing strips. Stony Man intel had discovered du Toit was holding off armament until his crew was in-country in order to facilitate quick hop times between intervening nations as the Super Puma flew into Banfora. Bolan had still been fearful that the men might have chosen to arm themselves with at least pistols in spite of du Toit's orders.

This appeared not to be the case. As Bolan raced toward Grimaldi and the waiting Cessna, he heard a burst of fire and knew du Toit had doubled back around the terminal's far corner. He realized he was lucky to have gotten even as much of a lead as he'd pulled off so far. He felt like cursing the rain and wind that had hampered his aim but held back as he knew it had hampered du Toit's aim, as well.

He caught a glimpse of a limp arm hanging out of the door of the helicopter. He saw two men covered with blood lying unmoving and facedown in the muck. Past them Bolan saw wounded men being helped by other mercenaries toward the edge of the airfield. He had hurt the South Africans. Not as bad as he'd hoped, but hurt them still.

There was a twin barking of pistols and, despite the wind, Bolan felt the shock wave as du Toit's rounds tore past him.

Bolan spun as he ran, sliding in the mud and throwing himself flat into the wet earth. He stretched out his pistol and fired back toward the terminal where du Toit knelt by the corner, his back to Bolan's original observation and ambush hide among the acacia trees. Du Toit fired again, and Bolan heard the rounds strike the fuselage of Grimaldi's plane, dimpling the airframe.

Bolan returned fire, squeezing off a careful burst. The girl stood on the ground between Bolan and du Toit. She simply stood unmoving in the rain as both men tried to fire around her. Bolan forced himself to look away and to concentrate on du Toit, but the girl's eyes tracked him like lasers.

On his feet again, Bolan pulled his shot to the left of the girl, still trying to throw off du Toit's aim. He whirled and raced for the plane. Bolan heard du Toit's guns go off again and ahead of him Grimaldi started the plane rolling.

Bolan shoved the Beretta into his shoulder sling and reached out for the rope ladder Grimaldi had kicked over the lip of the aircraft door. He grabbed hold with first one strong hand and then the other. He could no longer hear du Toit's firing over the plane's racing engines. Grimaldi saw that he was on the ladder, and Bolan felt the plane pick up speed as he clung to the dangling rope structure.

Bolan hauled himself up the ladder as the Cessna began to sprint down the muddy landing strip. He looked back and saw du Toit racing after him, both pistols blazing in the rain. The girl stood still, only her head moving as she tracked the fleeing plane's progress.

The Executioner reached the top of the ladder as Grimaldi pulled the nose of the plane airborne. The Executioner tumbled inside and yanked the ladder in after himself. He stood in the doorway and looked down as the airfield disappeared beneath him. The rain was falling too hard for him to see clearly, and he was soaked to the bone with it. Angry at the missed opportunity, Bolan grabbed the door and slammed it shut.

"Saragossa had better damn well be worth this," he muttered.

8

Du Toit lowered his pistols and watched the plane taking off into the storm.

Rain beat into his upturned face, and he fairly shook with the energy required to suppress his anger. He turned and looked at the girl before spitting on the ground, then he examined his helicopter, his beloved Super Puma.

The cargo bay was a slaughterhouse. Du Toit turned away, disgusted. His stomach was twisted in knots. Not again, he thought. He stalked away from the carnage of the ambush toward the terminal building. Bile was sour in his mouth.

A few years earlier du Toit had been part of a small mercenary force headed for Malabo, Equatorial Guinea, to initiate a coup. Instead, the mercenaries were taken at an airport in Zimbabwe while onboard their Boeing 727, awaiting the loading of weapons and equipment.

Du Toit had spent eighteen months incarcerated in Chikurubi Prison, where high tides frequently submerged the first floor with filthy water. He would die before he would go back to another African prison.

As du Toit walked, he grabbed his sat phone and punched in numbers.

"This is du Toit," he said when the other end was picked up. "We've had a snag," he stated.

Du Toit went on to tell his contact what had occurred, using curt, clipped tones.

"Tell the principal that an intelligence intercept must have happened on their end. If it had been an African or UN based leak it would have been a regiment of Burkina police who stopped us. A single operator using tight coordination air support? That's Western capabilities only. There isn't a military or secret service on this whole continent capable of this, besides us or our associates. You tell him he screwed it. Double the price, and tell him to get me operational funds to the bank in Ouagadougou immediately."

Du Toit stopped and turned, holding the sat phone to his ear. The girl had started to wander in his direction, a blank indifferent look on her face. He ignored her.

"We can still buy our way out of this problem," du Toit said into the phone. "Good, I'm glad to hear it. I'll be in contact shortly."

Du Toit looked at his vehicle and cursed when he realized it was completely unserviceable. It didn't matter, he realized, and some of the tension in him began to bleed away. As long as the international press didn't get wind of the situation, then money could make everything right in Burkina Faso. The third world nation wasn't so backward that bribes were useless.

"Get inside and sit down," du Toit suddenly said to the girl, speaking French.

He had to organize his men, secure medical evacuation for the wounded and eventually a cargo plane back to South Africa for the dead. He needed to uncrate and arm the men he had left before securing motorized transportation. He needed to get into town and pull money out of the transfer account he'd set up. He had to start bribing people, starting with Le Crème.

He looked up into the sky, turning his face into the deluge. He could see the face of the man who had ambushed him very clearly, each stark line and even the graveyard gaze of the man's cold blue eyes. He felt a grudging admiration. That feeling changed nothing. If he saw the man again, he'd kill him.

9

"That went well," Grimaldi said.

"About as well as could be expected."

Grimaldi pointed toward a laptop in a mesh pouch under the dash as Bolan slid into the copilot seat. Bolan picked it up and opened the screen. "What's this," he asked.

"Sitrep," Grimaldi answered. "Bear and Barb put it together based on a report from the NRO."

The National Reconnaissance Office was the division of the Department of Defense that designed, built and operated the reconnaissance satellites of the United States government. It also coordinated collection and analysis of information from airplane and satellite reconnaissance by the military services and the Central Intelligence Agency. It was funded through the National Reconnaissance Program, which was only one section of the National Foreign Intelligence Program.

Bolan began to click through the jpeg images, reading the synopses accompanying each photo. He was amazed by the detail and resolution of the satellite imagery, despite the heavy cloud cover from the tropical rains.

"How old are these?"

"I got 'em sent to me en route, that's up to the minute as of an hour ago. What do the troop movements look like?"

"Like Saragossa's screwed," Bolan said.

"Which means you're screwed."

"The MPCI is all over the township. They control it. There's a half-moon formation of Ivory Coast national army around the southern perimeter and a column of Burkina military bearing down from the north with field artillery and a handful of armored vehicles."

"Too hot?" Grimaldi asked. "The CIA can put a missile from a Predator drone through her front door if it comes down to it."

"In this weather?" Bolan asked.

Grimaldi simply nodded. Their own plane was being buffeted mercilessly as the Stony Man pilot tried to climb above the storm. Rain lashed the windshield, obscuring vision and, at the same time, maverick air currents snapped the transport plane's pitch with casual power.

"That's my point, Sarge. You want to jump in this? The meteorologist predicted a window in the rains for right now. There ain't no damn window."

"Weathermen." Bolan shrugged.

"It's your call, Sarge, just like always."

"The storm is strong, but low. We climb up above the storm and I jump from high and sail into the storm once I'm almost directly over target. I should only be exposed to the weather for three to five hundred feet."

"The wind is pretty calm down lower," Grimaldi allowed. "The clouds are simply sitting over the area, pissing a storm. These air currents are much higher."

"See? Easy as pie," Bolan said.

Bolan began applying camouflage greasepaint and Jack Grimaldi barked a laugh that echoed like a gunshot in the cockpit.

TAKING HIS HEAVY BACKPACK in both hands, Bolan heaved it up and muscled it before him. He shuffled forward, climbing up off his knees and making it to his feet. The black of the nighttime sky appeared out the open rectangular door of the Cessna.

Bolan hobbled ungracefully down the aisle and closer to the door. Suddenly the plane hit an air pocket and lurched. He hit the floor of the plane hard enough to knock the breath from his lungs, and he gasped. Then the Cessna twisted hard as it rolled through the turbulence. The motion lifted Bolan, backpack and all, about four inches off the deck. For one surreal moment Bolan simply levitated.

Then the Cessna rotated again and threw Bolan out into the night sky four miles above the ground.

The ice-cold slipstream punched into Bolan like a freight train. He spun off and away from the airplane. Like a turtle caught on the beach Bolan struggled to flip himself onto his stomach. He looked at his altimeter and saw it reading nineteen thousand feet.

Bolan reached for the ripcord on his parachute. He pulled the cord and felt the parachute separate. He was jerked sharply to a stop and then bounced. He saw the dark silhouette of Grimaldi's plane disappear above and behind him.

Bolan felt the force of the wind suddenly crack like a whip, and he began to plummet downward at an even faster rate. He looked up, startled, as his chute flared out like a Roman candle above him, useless.

Bolan felt the flesh of his face rippling under the force of rushing air. He blinked behind his visor and looked around. It was still too dark for him to make out any of the landscape details beneath him. The drop had been planned as a High Altitude High Opening, or HAHO, operational jump. He was to have pulled at approximately eighteen thousand feet and then sailed about three miles down onto his drop zone.

Still groggy from the brutally concussive force of the high winds, Bolan looked over at his altimeter again. He squinted, trying to read it. The needle was on fourteen thousand feet.

Bolan looked up at his parachute. The sail had completely collapsed and simply fluttered like a flag behind him as he plummeted toward the ground.

Operating on adrenaline and muscle memory, Bolan forced himself into action. Cold wind snapped into him, slapping him hard as he performed a cutaway, jettisoned the streaming, damaged canopy and then resumed his freefall.

For long moments Bolan fell, using the position of his body to surf the wind away from the possibility of entanglement with the damaged parachute. He reached down and across before grasping the handle of his reserve chute's cord handle firmly. He counted slowly and then yanked the cord.

As before, Bolan felt it separate perfectly and unfold above him smoothly. It snapped him short and then bounced him as the silk cells filled with air. Below him Bolan's backpack snapped on the end of its connector line. He was outfitted with nearly one hundred pounds of equipment, which could be a considerable liability in the thin altitude of the high jump.

Suddenly Bolan started falling faster and began spinning in and out of a semicontrolled corkscrew. He looked up and saw that crosswinds had collapsed one of the cells on his parasail. Then the canopy collapsed into a fissure, and Bolan began to plummet in earnest straight into the darkness below him.

Bolan reached up with both hands and gripped the parachute guides. He yanked on the lines, but the wind was cruel, fighting angrily against the falling man. Bolan clawed at his guides, falling faster and faster.

The Executioner heaved with every ounce of power in his body and finally he saw a chute cell on the left side fill with air, slowing his descent. He yanked again and the one next to it filled as well. His hurtling descent slowed to a more manageable speed, and he started to spiral in wide, lazy circles.

For a moment, exhausted, Bolan hung from his harness. The cold air felt frigid against his sweat-soaked body, and his stomach was clenched into tight knots. He forced himself to relax and expelled air in smooth pushes through his nose until his heart rate slowed to a more manageable tempo.

Bolan double-checked his altimeter and saw he was at slightly more than ten thousand feet. He keyed the display on the navigation device beside the altimeter on his wrist. His GPS reading blinked. He flipped his wrist over and took a reading on the compass set in the wristband. He used it to adjust his course and began parasailing toward the original drop zone.

The ground was two miles below him and obscured by angry black clouds. He was close to ten miles from his target. Once he had adjusted, Bolan reached up and heaved once again on his line. Another section of chute filled with air and flared out. But try as he might, he could not get the complete parachute to deploy properly, and he decided not to waste any more energy on the stubborn device.

Bolan looked around him, frowning. As he sailed down, heavy clouds rushed into view and he began working his faulty parachute into long, looping maneuvers designed to eat up speed before he made contact with the ground. Beneath him the rough topography expanded. He saw the strip of road he had picked out from the satellite imagery for his drop zone. The grassland was a smear of gray punctuated by scrubby trees.

Bolan scanned for any sign of patrols. As he sailed in toward the road, rain lashed at him and, as he made his final approach, he changed his movement into tighter, more circular corkscrew patterns. The tighter circles ate up even more vertical speed and would allow for a softer and more precise landing on the dirt road.

He picked out a spot with an invitingly wide section of road between the hidden and possibly treacherous ground of the grasslands on one side and a copse of acacia trees on the other. He began expertly guiding his chute in toward it. Bolan's left side suddenly dropped with a snapping motion. He craned his neck and looked up. He saw one of his few remaining cells collapse. Then the cell next to it developed a fissure and collapsed, folding inward on itself all over again.

Bolan hurtled toward the earth, slowed by only a single, uncollapsed cell in his parachute. He looked down, realizing he could no longer direct his chute or his imminent landing. He was falling too fast, dropping and spinning completely out of control. Bolan felt adrenaline rush his system. He knew he was going to miss the road and be thrown into the dense copse beyond it.

He reached down and unsnapped the emergency release at his waist, letting his heavy pack fall away below him. The effect was immediately noticeable, and his speed tempered though he still rushed down into the trees at a deadly pace. Bolan reached up with both hands and clawed at the guides of his single inflated cell.

Bolan bent himself almost double as he hauled on his lines, trying to twist his direction of fall away from the trees and back onto the road. For one wild second he thought he was going to make it and his body swung in a compact turn.

Then his boots struck treetops and the final cell of the parachute collapsed.

"WHY ARE YOU DRAGGING HER along?" Le Crème demanded.

Du Toit looked out the back window where rains beat down the elephant grass. "She's bought and paid for, what do you care?" he asked.

Le Crème shrugged, his left eye squinty and bloodshot. He fired up a cigar and shifted in the front seat of the Land Rover the Burkina national gendarme used as patrol vehicles. "I don't. Just curious."

"You and the cat."

Le Crème looked out the front windshield. The vehicle the two men shared rode at the front of a short convoy containing what was left of the South African mercenaries and a squadron of gendarme troopers purchased in Banfora as part of a massive bribe to Le Crème. It was imperative to defusing the situation with the MPCI rebels that Le Crème, in his uniform, make the initial contact.

Du Toit turned and looked at the girl. He couldn't remember her name, then realized he'd never bothered to ask. He didn't see any reason to do so now. He settled back into his seat.

The rains had turned the road to mud, and the ride was far from smooth. That he had been forced to break operational cover and enlist the open aid of a man like Le Crème galled du Toit. He reached into his pocket and pulled out a handful of antacid tablets. He popped them into his mouth one at a time, grinding the chalky medicine between his teeth.

"Colonel, forgive me," du Toit said. "The attack on my men has put me in a foul mood. What is the word from Yendere?"

"MPCI units are in the city. The rains have made the roads so impassible that our army units are forced to advance on foot. The commanders refuse to do so because it would mean leaving the artillery and heavier vehicles behind."

"They're leaving the MPCI to the Ivory Coast nationals?"

"Forward reconnaissance has reported that the monsoon has rendered the enemy army's own field pieces ineffective. Without artillery cover the Ivory Coast infantry has refused to advance on the rebels in their positions. For now we have a stalemate. Which is good for you, no?"

"Absolutely." Inwardly du Toit was disgusted anew. It was du Toit's opinion that, with the fall of apartheid, any military organization of worth on the African continent had become extinct.

10

Bolan crashed through the canopy of acacia trees like a camouflaged Icarus.

As he fell, thick branches flipped him back and forth, battering his back and limbs. Bolan struck a thick bole with his shoulder and spun off it. Leaves and branches slapped his face with stinging blows. Still spinning, Bolan hit another branch with his chest and bounced backward. The hard ground rushed up toward him.

This is it, he thought.

Bolan was stopped short with a brutal snap. He gasped as his parachute harness cinched up tight into his groin, and his spine arched painfully. His head snapped to the side from the whiplash force, and a blinding flash of light filled his eyes though they were squeezed tight shut.

Bolan slowly opened his eyes. He looked up and followed his lines to where they disappeared into the foliage above him. He reached out and tentatively explored the guides to see how secure his perch was. They hung taut where they carried his body weight against the point where the canopy hung up in the interwoven branches of the tree.

As Bolan wrapped his fingers around the lines in an exploratory grip, there was a ripping sound and the bottom fell out from under him. He dropped straight down another ten feet before being jerked to a stop as the canopy hung up again.

Bolan snarled a curse, part anger, part fear and mostly amazement that he was still alive and conscious after a jump like the one he had just made. He looked down between his dangling boots and saw the ground still fifteen feet below him. He turned his head and looked at the lattice of branches around him. He was stuck out into space about eight feet from the nearest tree trunk.

Bolan put his hand up to his mouth and bit into the leather tip of his glove, pulling his hand free. He spit the glove out and let it fall. Moving as quickly as he dared, he reached down to the cargo pocket of his black fatigues.

"Saragossa better be worth it," he repeated to himself.

He came out of the pocket with a nylon cord secured to a D-ring carabiner. He withdrew the rappel cord from his pocket like a stage magician coaxing an unending series of silk scarves from his sleeve. Bolan eyeballed a likely branch and flipped the carabiner over it. He snapped the cord through the gate, then ran a double loop through each of the two D-rings attached to his parachute harness suspenders.

Bolan payed out a little cord and then secured it with a fist he dug into the back of his hip, just under the curve of his buttock. He reached across his chest with his free hand and grasped the handle of a sheath knife hanging inverted from the suspender of his web gear.

Holding himself secure with his rappel cord, Bolan reached up and sliced the guidelines to the entangled chute. His body dropped as the last line was cut, and the nylon rappel cord stretched to take his weight. Free of the hung-up chute, Bolan sheathed the knife.

Holding himself steady, Bolan unbuckled his jump helmet

and let it fall. He cocked his head, straining to listen for any sound. The falling rain drowned out everything in its monotonous rhythm. Even inside the tangle of tree branches the rain was fierce and invasive.

Bolan lifted his fist straight out to his side from its anchor at his hip and let the nylon cord pay through his gloved hand. The friction was instantaneous, but the drop was short and Bolan completed his rappel quickly. He sagged at the knees as he landed to absorb the slight impact and quickly disengaged from his parachute harness and rappel cord.

Speed was of the essence. This side of the landscape was farthest from the commercial installations, and reconnaissance had suggested it was only thinly monitored with Burkina security forces focused on gaining the high ground, such as it was, above the village of Yendere and the perimeter defenses around the township itself.

Bolan reached under his arm and pulled the silenced Beretta 93-R from a shoulder holster. He wore his Desert Eagle on his thigh as well. Secured to his backpack was a Mk 48 light machine gun along with several collapsible LAWS rocket launchers. In addition, Bolan also carried a bayonet, boot knife, piano wire garrote and a selection of hand grenades.

Hurriedly, Bolan gathered up his discarded gear and the loose end of the rappel cord. He moved over to the tree trunk and secured everything in the hollow of a branch. It would not fool an alert, experienced tracker, but it might go unnoticed by a more casual observer in such weather. Bolan realized he was breathing through his mouth, almost panting like a dog in the choking heat and humidity. His priority was to find his backpack.

In addition to his weapons, Bolan's pack carried tools for

breaching obstacles, surreptitious entry, electronic and digital interdiction, night navigation and, as a last resort, satellite communications. The operation had called for his infiltration solo, and as a result he had been forced to carry the wide range of equipment and accessories that had compromised his ease of movement and the parachute drop.

Bolan checked the Beretta. He used his thumb to click the fire selector switch off safety. He moved out of the copse of trees and began to push through the tall purple and yellow grass toward the strip of road where he had been forced to dump his bag. Though it seemed to make more sense to avoid a potential population center like a road, it had been a much safer bet than jumping into the unknown of the tall elephant grass. Of course his careful planning had been for nothing, but a deserted strip of dirt road was still a much better objective than dropping blind into the potential dangers of unseen ground where a broken ankle or neck could end his mission before it had scarcely begun.

As Bolan pushed toward the road, the wind died down and the rain began to fall even harder. His fatigues were quickly soaked, but his boots did a good job of repelling the water as he kicked through the grass. It was feverishly hot despite the constant rainfall.

He held the Beretta up and ready as he moved toward the road, using his free hand to part the ten-foot blades of grass before he took each step. He realized that with the rain muting sound and the thick grass reducing vision to easily under six feet, a firefight in such an environment would be chaotic and close quarters to the extreme.

Bolan pushed through a stubborn clump of hairy leafed foliage and suddenly found he was at the road. To either side of the dirt thoroughfare ran an area of shorter grass, a yard or two at most wide. In the middle of the road stood an old model military jeep, its engine idling and headlights on. Three men in Burkina national army uniforms stood in a loose circle around Bolan's backpack, which lay stuck in the mud. The men all held AK-74 assault rifles, and the soldier on the far right utilized a drum attachment instead of the standard banana clip magazine.

Bolan cursed silently in frustration. Officially Burkina Faso enjoyed friendly relations with the United States. The truth was that the former army captain and current president was a corrupt leader with an expansionist mind-set well suited to head the government of thugs he commanded. There had been no way a third-world nation as rife with corruption as the government in Ouagadougou was could be trusted with an operation as covert as the one Bolan was attempting. The fact that the UN delegates of the U.S. and Burkina Faso could speak pleasantly of deals and of the necessity of keeping Islamic extremists from gaining influence in West Africa did not mean the soldiers and police of the nation did not have greedy, bloodstained hands. The president was completely unaware of the operation being undertaken beneath the nose of his security services.

Because of this, the Executioner was an armed insurgent in a foreign country as sensitive to memories of marauding ex-colonial, white mercenaries as any other African nation. At best Bolan could expect arrest and prison while the U.S. government disavowed any knowledge of him. Worse would be the torture for information he either didn't have or would never reveal. Worst of all would be a summary execution at the hands of a national army facing invasion by hostile forces.

Bolan felt rain running in rivulets down his face. In the distance he saw a flash of light, then heard the staccato thunder of an artillery barrage. The soldiers standing over Bolan's pack looked toward the sound. It was hard to see their faces clearly through the falling rain, but they looked very young. They scattered quickly into the grass on the far side of the road.

The equipment contained in the bag at their feet was untraceable and commercial for the most part. It was also expensive and advanced, not the sort of thing normally carried by ragtag insurgents or even by the most elite units of the small Ivory Coast army, if such a unit could even be said to exist. Such gear turned over to the African Council or the UN was a potentially explosive political hot potato. Bolan exhaled slowly through his nose and lifted the silenced Beretta. He had to retrieve the pack.

Bolan knew that the civil war across the border in Ivory Coast was not a simple affair of good and evil. Like most conflicts on the continent it was filled with ambiguity. In the end it was, like most bush wars, a matter of tribal loyalties. Ivory Coast had been brutal to its population in its antiinsurgent campaign. By the same token the MPCI had proved themselves just as savage and bloodthirsty and the war crimes attributed to them every bit as horrific as the worst of its enemy: mutilation, torture, murder, rape, looting and wholesale destruction.

The reason the MPCI had been able to exist was due, in large part, to men like the ones Bolan had seen on the road. The Burkina army provided a safe haven for the MPCI, allowing them to escape the guns of the Ivory Coast national army and dragging out the conflict while the government in Ouagadougou sought to exploit the carnage and bloodshed to its own advantage.

Bolan wasn't sure there were any good guys in this battle. The Executioner approached his pack as quickly and quietly as he could. He dragged the heavy bag across the muddy road. He was almost back to the elephant grass when someone opened fire on him.

Bolan's pistol spit muted flame from the muzzle of the suppressor. The soldier armed with the drum magazine in his Kalashnikov assault rifle folded at the knees. His head jerked oddly, and then he dropped straight over onto the road.

His two companions rushed from the grass firing wildly. Bolan's next bullet caught the soldier standing to the left of his first target in the side of the head. Even across the distance in the rain, Bolan saw the flash of bone fragments as the man's skull came apart. The man's black beret went flying, and he was bowled straight over onto the corpse of his dead brother in arms.

The last soldier yelped in shock, his face splashed with the hot blood of his friend. He whirled and brought up his assault rifle. He triggered a wild burst as he spun and 5.45 mm rounds shattered the windshield of the jeep.

Bolan smoothly drew down on the man as he spun and caught him high on the left shoulder by his neck. The 9 mm Parabellum round punched into the soldier and halted his spin. The man looked up instinctively and caught the outline of Bolan as the Executioner crouched in the elephant grass. The Beretta spit a final time.

The man's head snapped up and back, and he backpedaled under the impact. His feet tangled up in the slack legs of the other soldiers and he flopped over backward to land on top of the pile of corpses the Executioner had just created with cool precision and unshakable will.

Bolan stepped fully out of the tall grass and onto the muddy apron beside the dirt road. He checked up and down the road in both directions but saw no other potential threats. He knew the sound of the weapons fire was a potential complication.

It was probable, due to the location of Bolan's drop zone to the forming battlefield, that the Burkina team was simply a rear security patrol. The very real possibility remained that the men were the vanguard of a troop column sweeping the flank of the incursion forces as well. That meant many more of their number could be in the immediate vicinity.

Bolan moved to the back of the jeep and pulled a five-gallon can of gas out of the rear. He walked around the front of the vehicle and began to pour the fuel on the bodies. It was an unpleasant necessity.

If there were more troops in the area, then it was very likely they would have an officer. American Special Forces soldiers had been active in the region recently, training forces in Mali. It was imperative that he make the Burkina army believe that some forward element of Ivory Coast incursion forces had caught these soldiers in an ambush.

Bolan pulled a lighter out of a secure pocket, then bent and lit the gasoline. The puddle caught with a vicious whoosh and began to burn, despite the rainfall.

Turning his back on the funeral pyre he had just created, Bolan moved on to the jeep. He unhooked a fragmentation grenade and took a coil of fishing line from a pocket in his pants. Holding the grenade in one hand, Bolan placed the heavy line in his mouth and fished a roll of electrician's tape free of a pocket. He opened the driver's door and quickly went to work.

When finished, Bolan scooped up his pack, secured his main weapon and pushed off the road and into the elephant grass. Behind him the falling rain slapped down the flames of his bonfire, causing greasy black smoke to hug the muddy, blood-splattered road.

11

"What the hell is this?" Le Crème suddenly demanded.

Du Toit looked up, snapping out of the reverie the drive south into the interior had placed him in. The windshield wipers on the Land Rover were working furiously to keep up with the downpour. The sound of rubber on glass was rhythmic and annoying.

Through the rain, in the glow of the vehicle's headlights, du Toit got a glimpse of a military jeep pulled off to one side of the dirt road. He leaned forward as Le Crème's driver slowed. Beyond the Burkina vehicle lay a huddled mass of what appeared to be partially charred corpses.

"Stop!" Le Crème commanded.

"Could be an ambush," du Toit pointed out, bringing up his submachine gun.

Le Crème ignored him and drew his sidearm. "Deploy the men in a perimeter around the convoy," he ordered his driver and sergeant. The driver threw the Land Rover into park and jumped out of the vehicle.

He took his AKM with him and began shouting instructions at the truck directly behind Le Crème's vehicle. Armed gendarmes poured out of the back of the truck and took up positions along the side of the road.

The girl shifted in her seat and du Toit turned to look at her. For the first time he witnessed some sort of reaction from the teenager. She leaned forward eagerly, trying to see the bodies in the road.

"You never see dead people before?" du Toit demanded. He threw open his door and stuck a leg out. His trouser leg was instantly soaked by the torrential downpour.

"Is it him?" the girl asked. "Did he kill them?"

Du Toit didn't have to ask whom she meant. He felt a flash of unreasonable anger. As if of its own volition, his hand flew up and he struck the girl across her mouth. The girl's head rocked back, and blood was smeared like paint across her full lips. She did not cry out.

Du Toit felt a sudden rush of arousal and snarled. He finished climbing out of the Land Rover and slammed the door so hard the frame rocked on the suspension. He stomped through the mud and walked around the abandoned military vehicle. He came up behind Le Crème, who stood over the pile of corpses, looking down on them.

"MPCI?" du Toit asked.

"Who else?"

The mercenary narrowed his eyes against the rain and looked down at the remains in the mud. Mutilation of corpses was hardly newsworthy in Africa. He squatted for a closer look. Behind him Le Crème shouted at a subordinate to check the jeep.

Du Toit looked away from the disfiguring crack in the top man's forehead. A single pistol round—he'd seen enough wounds to be able to identify them, even if he wasn't a forensic specialist. Hell, he'd put enough pistol rounds into the heads of dissidents in South African townships to know the wounds by rote.

He looked at the next man and frowned. Same single

round to the forehead. Du Toit reached down and grabbed hold of the top man's shirt. Ignoring how the burned fabric smeared across his hands, du Toit shoved the dead Burkina soldier aside.

Behind him a gendarme opened the door to the vehicle.

Du Toit put the heel of his palm against the second dead man in the pile and rudely shoved the corpse out of the way. Charcoaled skin clung to du Toit's hand as the body slid off to the side. The South African could clearly see the third man at the bottom of the pile.

An untidy third eye had been opened in the man's forehead. Realization struck du Toit like a sucker punch. Three men, armed with assault rifles, taken down by single pistol shots to the head. That was some heavy duty killing, coldly, professionally accurate and detached. It sure wasn't any MPCI child-soldier hopped up on drugs.

"Shit," du Toit whispered.

The jeep exploded behind him with a loud bang, and he jumped. He stood and whirled, bringing up his submachine gun. Beside him Le Crème swore and gendarmes began shouting frantically. Du Toit eyed his own men, who kept their weapons and eyes trained on the tall grass to the front of their positions.

Du Toit looked toward the scene of the detonation. A gendarme was down. The grenade shrapnel had blown out the vehicle's already cracked windshield and the driver's window from the inside. It had ripped the gendarme's chest open like a buzz saw. The heat of the grenade had set the man's uniform on fire, and it flared briefly before the rain saturated it. Inside the cab-seat stuffing smoldered.

A frightened Burkina soldier began to spray the grass wildly with automatic weapon fire. Du Toit snarled in frustration and sprang forward. He struck the back of the panicked soldier's head with the butt of his submachine gun, dropping the man instantly. Du Toit spun back toward La Crème.

"It was a booby trap!" du Toit snarled. "Only a booby trap. Calm them down!"

Le Crème began shouting orders at the gendarmes while du Toit ordered his men back into their vehicles. Cold hate filled him, calming his anger and feeding him energy like high-voltage electricity into a transformer. Du Toit turned back toward Le Crème's Land Rover.

He reached out and snapped open the door. He ducked and stuck his head into the back of the car where the girl sat looking at the ruined flesh of the gendarme through her passenger window.

"You like it?" he asked. "You like what he did?" Du Toit let his subgun rest on its sling and reached out. He hauled the girl to him, grabbing her with one hand by the hair and twisting her face up into his. Her expression blank, the girl looked up at him.

"You like it?" He felt crazed. "Then taste it!"

Du Toit shoved the palm of the hand covered with the dead soldier's burned flesh into the girl's face. Du Toit's teeth were clenched in a furious grimace, and his breathing was ragged in his own ears. He knew what he was feeling and he hated himself for it.

He was afraid.

Feeling futile, du Toit shoved the girl away. "I'm going to kill him," he promised her.

"He is *Gunab,* the death spirit," she whispered. "He can't be killed."

SARAGOSSA FIRED A BURST of harassing fire down the staircase. She stepped back through the doorway of her room and turned. There was no warning. The bullet struck her low in the gut and drove her back against the wall.

She was dimly aware then of the rifle report and knew someone had fired on her through the window from the rooftop of the mosque.

She dropped straight down on her behind, below the sight line of the window. Her hand went to her wound, and blood poured out between her fingers. She looked down, gasping at the pain, and realized she had been hurt badly.

The wound was mortal and she had no illusions about it.

She slid along the floor until she could prop her back against the wall directly under the window. She waved away the flies. They had appeared when she wasn't paying attention. Driven under the eaves and indoors by the rain, the smell of blood and decaying flesh had drawn them to her room quickly. Now they were thick in the place, and her own blood was adding to the buffet.

She needed to dress the wound, she realized, stanch the bleeding before she was past the point of no return. It hurt to move, and each breath was an agony. She decided to rest. Just for a minute. Just long enough to catch her breath.

12

Bolan pushed his way through the towering grass. He moved quickly to put as much distance between himself and the scene of the ambush as he could. For the first leg of his march he didn't need to reference his navigational equipment. He knew from the satellite photography exactly what compass reading the copse of acacia trees had been in relation to the road. He began to move as fast as he could through the soaking wet terrain.

After a while the repetition of his movements set in and he began to break trail with efficiency, catching his stride and making good time across the grassland. He would take several steps, push through a stand of grass, then take several more steps before repeating the procedure. It was hard work in the oppressive heat and humidity.

Bolan pushed aside a thick clump of grass and froze. The moment stretched out in time as adrenaline flooded his body. He felt raindrops, as warm as blood, splash his face. The heat was like a wet blanket smothering him, and his chest heaved as he fought to fill his lungs with the balmy air.

He saw the Cape buffalo lift its big, flat head. A line of mucous ran in a thick rope from one cavern of a nostril. The horns were heavy and grew out in successive ridges to deadly points designed to fend off lions. The beast snorted, causing spittle and snot to fly as it lumbered to its feet.

"Easy," Bolan said.

The animal stood about five and a half feet tall at the shoulder and was easily fifteen hundred pounds. Behind the first beast others in its little herd began to rise out of the tall grass where they were bedded down to shelter from the rain. The breeze shifted slightly, and their musk and the stink of their dung was suddenly cloying.

Bolan knew that along with the hippopotamus, Cape buffalo were considered one of the most dangerous animals in Africa due to their unpredictable and aggressive temperaments. They had been known to ambush hunters who became confused in the tall grass of the savanna. Their sense of smell was uncanny and compensated for both poor hearing and eyesight. They were far more suited to a struggle in the tall grass during the rain and at night than Bolan.

He lifted his Mk 48 up as he backed away slowly. He didn't want to advertise his presence by firing bursts of machine-gun fire at charging buffalo, but the animal might not give him a choice. The bull snorted again and stood motionless, watching as Bolan carefully stepped backward into the tall grass.

Like the beads of a hanging curtain the blades of grass closed in behind Bolan, obscuring him from view. He slowly exhaled. The wind was coming into his face from the direction of the herd and once the grass obscured him from the bull, Bolan hoped he'd become functionally invisible to it.

He twisted slowly so as not to overbalance himself under the weight of his heavy pack. He parted more stalks of thick grass drenched from the rain. He brought the Mk 48 up to port arms and turned a shoulder against the oppressive blades of grass as he stepped away. His plan was to backtrack away, then loop wide around the area in hopes of avoiding the herd.

The bull bawled out an angry roar as it suddenly crashed through the grass. It came from Bolan's left and was charging at nearly full speed by the time it broke through and ran him down. Bolan tried to twist and bring up the Mk 48, then realized he'd never complete the spin in time. He ducked a shoulder and tried to turn to take the impact with his backpack.

The maneuver was partially successful and certainly saved his life. A horn gored the pack as the enraged creature charged past. Furious at its entanglement, the running animal cut sharply and tossed its head. Bolan grunted at the sudden whiplash, and the light machine gun was ripped out of his hands.

He was thrown hard to the ground and felt the crushing weight of the buffalo drive into him as it sought to keep goring its prey. Bolan reached for his Beretta in its shoulder holster, but the weight of the animal was so massive that he couldn't reach the pistol butt where it was pressed hard against the soggy ground.

The animal twisted sharply and Bolan flipped over as his pack ripped open, spilling his gear and equipment across the grass. He landed hard, and his head snapped so sharply he saw stars. He managed to free one arm from the collapsing pack, and then the buffalo struck him again.

Bolan grunted under the force of the impact and felt himself being dragged across the grass at ridiculous speed as the enraged bull charged. He bent backward under the train-like force. He reached the butt of the Beretta and yanked it clear of the holster. Bolan twisted and reached up, grabbing hold of the wirelike hair running down the back of the buffalo's neck. He sank his fingers into the hair and made a tight fist.

He used the grip to anchor himself as he twisted up over the edge of the backpack where the beast's horns remained imbedded. Images flashed by—grass being whipped aside and other herd animals bounding to their feet in panic—as he clung to the charging beast. Bolan brought around the muzzle of the Beretta and jammed it into the thick column of muscle in the neck directly behind the animal's skull.

The Beretta fired a 3-round burst, and the animal's blood splashed Bolan's face, soaking his shirt. The Parabellum rounds crashed into the fist-sized vertebrae of the enraged buffalo and burrowed deep into the muscles of the creature's neck.

The effect was instantaneous. The bull's head dropped and its horns gouged into the rain-softened earth, digging deep furrows of grass roots and rich dirt before they caught and lodged tight. Bolan was flung straight down, the breath driven from his body as the bull's skull hammered into his torso. The horns caught, and the skidding beast flipped over them in a tangle of blood, legs and flesh.

The stench of spilled blood was like a bomb going off in the herd. Panicked animals began racing through the tall grass in every direction. Bolan could only react instinctively. The situation was unfolding too rapidly for coherent thought.

He flipped around and hugged up tight against the warm body of the buffalo he'd killed, using the gigantic corpse as a shield against the flailing hooves thundering around him. Bolan regained his composure quickly though his situation was beyond even his vast experience.

The sound and motion were overwhelming as the animals broke and crashed through the bush in an attempt to escape the stink of the blood of one of their own kind. Bolan remembered reading that the big animals converged in herds numbering from a few dozen to several thousand.

He had to assume that, caught between inhabited and built-up sectors, this patch of ground would be home to only a small herd. That would be more than enough to kill him if a flying hoof or tripped-up buffalo crashed into him. Twice, charging animals leaped over his position and a stream of them ran past where he lay huddled. The experience seemed to drag on forever.

It was over in less than a minute. Bolan sensed a passing of movement and then a lull in the frenzied sound. He looked up over the stomach of the dead animal. Grass lay flattened in huge swatches around him, but he saw no sign of any more buffalo.

Still gripping his pistol, Bolan stood. Blood smeared his face and caked his hair. The dense humidity made it difficult for him to catch his breath. He looked around and saw torn and broken equipment scattered across the trampled savanna.

He walked back several steps, scanning the ground for anything worth saving. He found his Mk 48 almost immediately. It had been trampled and broken in several places. The green plastic ammunition drum had been cracked open, and metallic cartridges spilled out across the wet, purple grass. Bolan picked up a tube from his combat harness and drank from the camel pouch on his back. He rinsed the taste of animal blood and his own disgust at the turn of events out of his mouth and spit onto the ground.

He looked at the monotonous wall of grass standing around him and shook away the nagging apprehension that at any moment some wild animal would crash through it and run him down again. He had a long history of living with fear, of coping with adrenaline highs that went on for days like elastic nightmares of blood and thunder. He forced himself to be calm, to a reorientation of his focus. What happened, no matter how incredible, had already happened. It was over. The operation still stretched out before him, just as critical as ever.

Bolan realized he was turned around by the incident. He pulled his compass out of a belt pouch and took a reading. Time was sliding away from him at every moment, and each setback cost him a little more of that precious, irretrievable commodity.

As Bolan set out again, he heard artillery fire off in the distance and picked out the flashes of rounds exploding on the horizon above the grass. The battle was directly in line with his compass bearing. Marie Saragossa lay in the heart of the battle.

Bolan began to move at a rapid pace through the grass. The outskirts of Yendere were less than a mile ahead of him. Intelligence had shown the road leading out of the village and toward Banfora had been clogged with refugees ahead of the MPCI guerrillas and the Ivory Coast army advance. The latest satellite imagery had revealed innumerable flashes of automatic weapon fire and new craters from artillery pieces.

Bolan didn't understand why Saragossa had hunkered down instead of making her way to Banfora, or even Ouagadougou ahead of the combat. It made him apprehensive of what he would find once he had infiltrated the border village of Yendere.

No longer hampered by his heavy pack and larger weapon, Bolan covered the mile or so between him and the village in just under a half an hour, breaking trail the entire way. It had been a grueling forced march, but when Bolan broke the grass line he found himself placed almost exactly where he'd aimed when laying out his compass readings earlier.

The landscape was reduced to a monochromatic dark gray by the continuous deluge. Bolan crawled up to the cover of a lone acacia tree and parted the grass, peering out at the village before him. He was sore and tender from his rough parachute jump, and it had only been exacerbated by his meeting with the buffalo. He was worried that if he remained motionless for too long he would stiffen up and lose some of his reflex speed, a potential deadly turn of events.

He carefully scrutinized the cluster of buildings and plowed fields below him. Yendere's buildings were typically dried mud architecture with lines of rectangular houses punctuated by round structures used to store grain. The largest building was a walled mosque, despite the fact that most of the population was traditionally animist.

Bolan marked the building because of that. If neither side was likely to attach a religious significance to the large structure, it became the strongest defensive point in the township. The second point would be the Kibidwe Hotel across the center street from it. Bolan frowned. The hotel was the last known location of Saragossa.

The township had been home to several hundred people and was a rural center for produce, raw cotton collection, and trade commerce with village merchants making the arduous trip to Banfora to return with goods. There was a school, a medical clinic, a UNICEF office and a strip of small businesses, including a mechanic shop and several dozen of the stalls commonly used for selling local produce. Those structures consisted of four to six wooden posts holding up tin or thatch roofs and were open air with heavy tables often placed in their centers to display goods and materials.

No one moved openly on the streets, and more than one of the buildings smoldered in the rain. Three or four ancient cars were strewed across the road into town, riddled with bullets. From his vantage point Bolan could make out a shoeless corpse lying in the middle of a street, the man's stomach was already distended from pent-up decomposition gases.

Burkina Faso was among the three or four poorest nations on the planet. More than ninety percent of the population engaged in subsistence agriculture, allowing little time for other industrial output. Much of the male population migrated to other countries in the region to perform work for months at a time before returning to their homeland.

Regional commerce centers like Yendere were vital strategic choke points for the Burkina Faso economy. The loss of even one economic center in the province could spell tangible hardship for the rest of the nation.

Bolan looked out through the rain, his mind worrying at the problem of what Venezuela's government could possibly want in such a dirt-poor African nation.

Between Bolan and the village center was a cemetery. Several stray artillery rounds had struck the ancient field and torn up the ground. Coffins were ripped loose from the earth, leaving bodies and skeletons strewed around the muddy field. The turned-up earth still remained a darker color than the topsoil despite the heavy rains. There had been a battle here, and recently. Bolan scanned through the structures and thatched roof stalls out toward the edges of the grassland and gently rising hills. He detected no movement.

Burkina Faso had a typical, low caliber and poorly trained military better at intimidation of civilians than sustained combat operations. He strongly doubted them capable of the noise-and-light discipline necessary to maintain a modern complex ambush. It would be foolish to underestimate any enemy at this point, however.

Beyond the township on three sides stretched fields and pastureland. Shallow irrigation canals cut through the cultivated land and against one side of the built-up urban area a large complex of now empty corrals had been erected to house sheep during the shearing season. Bolan began linking a path of cover and concealment from his present point to his target area the same way an experienced rock climber mapped out a technical route up a cliff face from one secure handhold to the next.

Using the headstones of the cemetery, Bolan would make his way to the irrigation canals and exploit their cover up to the animal pens, where he could then approach the back door to the hotel through a labyrinth of alleyways. The area was open, and until he reached the alleys and narrow streets of Yendere proper he would be at a distinct and deadly disadvantage to anyone with a long weapon.

Bolan drew his Desert Eagle. If he took fire moving toward the township there would be little need for the stealthy Beretta. His accuracy with the big handgun was unparalleled.

Bolan took a long last scan of the topography before moving out. He saw no motion other than the falling deluge and heard nothing but the white noise of the driving rain. He wiped water out of his face and moved out from the cover of the acacia tree.

13

Du Toit looked away from the window and frowned. He'd come to an important realization. As a mercenary, he had made a career out of hunting and killing poorly trained African nationals whom he'd almost always outgunned. In his heart du Toit knew he had never faced a man like the killer at the Banfora airport.

God help me, he thought. For the first time in a long time du Toit was afraid.

Outside the Land Rover the rain suddenly stopped. Du Toit wondered when the mystery man would strike again.

BOLAN MOVED IN A CROUCH through the Yendere graveyard.

He wove in and out of headstones, skirting graves torn open by artillery rounds. He averted his gaze from the mummified husks of old corpses and tried not to step on any of the skeletal remains that lay scattered about like children's toys.

The rain fell steadily. Bolan remained a ghostly figure as he traversed the cemetery. The weight of the Desert Eagle was reassuring in his hand. He breathed in the humid air, pushing his body through his exertion.

The first rifle crack was muted and distant. Bolan dropped to one knee behind a headstone. Straining his ears against the muffling effect of the rain, he heard another single shot. A burst of submachine gun fire answered it, and Bolan saw the muzzle-flash flare out of the dark rectangle of a window in the second story of the old hotel.

Bolan quickly ascertained that none of the fire was being directed toward him. He was about fifty yards from the edge of the township, where thatch-and-mud hovels surrounded the more built-up areas in a loose ring broken at random by animal pens. Bolan wiped rainwater out of his eyes and looked toward the irrigation ditch that had been his original infiltration route.

He scowled. He wasn't bursting with anticipation to slide into the muddy, waist-deep water of the ditch. Another burst of submachine gun fire came from the hotel's second story and was answered by two controlled single shots.

Bolan made his decision.

He rose from behind the headstone and began moving toward the township proper, dodging the open graves, artillery craters and headstones like a track runner navigating hurdles on the quarter-mile track. The soaked ground swallowed up the impact of his footsteps, spraying dirty water with every step he took.

He reached the wall of a mud hovel and went around to one side. Peering around the edge, he saw an unpaved alley running deeper into the township. Bullet holes riddled the wall of one long, low mud-brick building. A mongrel dog lay sprawled, shot dead, in the weeds beside it.

Bolan pushed forward. The alley ran behind the hotel several blocks up. Garbage cans lay overturned in the muddy street, and rubbish was heaped in soggy piles everywhere. Bolan stayed in close to one side of the building and edged his way carefully into the street. His eyes squinted against the rain, searching windows and doorways for any sign of movement.

There was no more gunfire. The rain was even louder inside the built-up structures of the township. It hammered onto shanty roofs of corrugated tin and ran off into makeshift gutters, forming rushing waterfalls that splashed out into the street every few yards. Bolan blinked water from his eyes and stalked farther into the tangle of dank and twisting streets.

He crossed an open area between two one-story buildings and sensed motion. He spun, bringing up the Desert Eagle. A black-and-white goat on the end of a frayed rope looked up and bleated at him. The animal's fur was matted down from exposure to the rain. There was a little hutch built behind the staked-out goat. From the doorway of the hutch a slender black arm and hand sprawled in the mud. There was a bracelet of hammered copper around the delicate wrist, and the fingers had frozen in rigor mortis.

Bolan looked up the street in both directions but saw nothing. He crouched and reached across with his left hand to his right boot and pulled a Gerber Guardian straight blade from his boot sheath. He stepped into the pen, ignoring the squish of mud and dung in the sodden straw under his feet.

The animal bleated again and Bolan shushed it reflexively. He reached down and slid the double-edged blade into the loop of twine around the animal's neck. He flicked his wrist and severed the rope. The goat walked to the edge of the pen and began munching on the hay that had been out of its reach before.

Bolan slowly sank to one knee. He slid the knife back into its sheath and bent forward, looking into the hutch. The shadows were deep in the small space. The arm stretched back into the dark. Bolan blinked and the dark congealed into the shape of a woman.

She was young and dead, with opaque eyes staring out at him. There was a bloody, open gash where her throat had been.

As Bolan's eyes adjusted to the deeper gloom, he saw naked thighs under a pushed up, one-piece dress. He looked away.

Bolan rose slowly out of his crouch. He heard a man call out several streets over in a dialect Bolan couldn't understand. Someone answered. Anger made Bolan grit his teeth.

Constant exposure to violence and death numbed the human animal. It made him indifferent to the suffering of his fellow man, made pulling the trigger easier. Bolan had fought that dehumanizing demon for a long time.

He knew the men who had raped and murdered this woman were human, just like him. They killed people, just like him. But they were nothing like him.

Bolan secured his grip on the butt of his pistol.

He walked over to the edge of the animal pen between the two houses and looked out into the narrow street. The incessant rain made puddles jump with the weight of its falling drops. He opened a little gate and stepped out into the street.

He began to move toward the hotel, walking quickly with his weapon ready. He reached the edge of a round, one-story silo and looked carefully around it. A short passageway between buildings linked the main street with the secondary alley Bolan now navigated.

About twenty yards down a man stood with his back to Bolan. He held a SKS carbine at port arms. A machete was stuck through the back of a green web belt cinched around dirty, knee-length shorts. The African wore a dirty black T-shirt with sleeves cut off, and his head was covered with a filthy red bandanna. Ammunition belts were looped around his narrow shoulders in a loose X.

Bolan raised the Desert Eagle in a slow, smooth gesture. He straightened his arm and placed the sights squarely on the occipital lobe of the rebel soldier's skull. His finger curled around the trigger of the .44 Magnum and took up the slack.

The rebel looked to his left and lifted a fist above his head in some kind of signal.

Bolan shuffled sideways across the narrow mouth of the alley, his pistol tracking the man's back with every step. On the other side of the alley Bolan slid around a corner and put his back against the wall of a nondescript building. He eased the big .44 into the holster on his thigh.

He pressed his head against the wall and turned his face back toward the dirt lane he had just crossed, drawing the Beretta 93-R out in a even, deliberate motion. He held the pistol up so that the muzzle was poised beside the hard plane of his cheekbone. He bent slightly at the knee and crouched before risking a glance back around the edge of the building.

Another rebel soldier had joined the first. This one held an ancient French MAT-49 submachine gun, and together the two men jogged quickly up the alley toward Bolan's position. The big American ducked back around the edge of the building. He skipped several steps to the side and slid into the recessed arch of a doorway.

As the men rounded the corner, he could hear them talking to each other in low, excited voices. Both of them turned down the alley in the direction of the hotel and Bolan's hiding spot.

The Executioner stepped out of the doorway and into the rain. He lowered his pistol as the men stumbled up against each other in surprise at his sudden appearance. The silenced Beretta spit a single time as Bolan extended his arm. The rebel holding the MAT-49 went down. The rain had plastered the gunman's shirt to his skinny frame, and Bolan could clearly see where the soft-nosed 9 mm Parabellum round smashed into the prominent ridge of the man's sternum and punched through it.

The guerrilla fighter dropped his submachine gun, and it

fell across his legs as he struck the ground. Beside him the SKS-armed rebel struggled to bring his longer weapon to bear as Bolan swiveled at the hips and brought the Beretta around at point-blank range.

The man's eyes bulged in his terror. Bolan's round powered through his face at the bridge of the nose with a loud *smack* that sounded wet and sharp even in the falling rain.

The man sagged into the mud. The SKS carbine dropped from limp fingers and fell to the ground.

Even as the second rebel fell Bolan spun, Beretta ready and tracking for any more hostiles. He heard no alarm, saw no movement and took no fire. He quickly holstered the Beretta and went to one knee in the muck where the corpses were pouring blood from their ragged wounds.

He scooped up the SKS and checked the safety and breech. Satisfied, Bolan hooked it over his shoulder and across his torso by the sling. Then he picked up the squat little MAT-49 and looked it over. Once again satisfied with what he found, Bolan rose. He reached down with his left hand and snatched one of the rebels by his shirt collar.

Bolan dragged the body over to the edge of the narrow street and laid it against the building. He quickly returned to the center of the alley and retrieved the second gunman. He hauled the limp corpse over and threw it down by its brother against the building.

Looking around, Bolan spotted what he wanted. He looped the MAT-49 over one shoulder and grabbed an overturned garbage can. Without preamble he covered the bodies with soggy garbage and then placed the empty can in front of them. The camouflage would only pass the most rudimentary of inspections, but Bolan hoped that anyone simply looking down the alley in the rain and dark would miss the bodies.

Bolan took the MAT-49 into his hands and began to jog down the alley in the direction of the Hotel Kibidwe.

The hotel formed one side of the center square of the Yendere township. Forming another directly across from the hotel was the walled mosque of mud brick and the accompanying *madrassa,* or religious school. A long low building with the Burkina Faso flag hanging limply denoted where the official government offices shared space with UNICEF on yet a third side of the square. Either side of the street on the fourth side of the township square was taken up by the most prosperous of the village market vendors.

During Bolan's approach, more sporadic gunfire had sounded, triggering another burst from the hotel's second floor. The Executioner moved carefully toward the combination gas station and garage positioned beside the hotel across from the mosque. A mess of fifty-five-gallon oil drums had been placed haphazardly behind the building, and Bolan wound his way into these as he approached the structure.

Rainwater shimmered in oily rainbows on the lids of the barrels, and they felt greasy under his touch. A dim yellow bulb burned above the back door to the garage. The door sagged on its ancient hinges, and its paint peeled badly. The knob was burnished metal that looked slick from the continuous rainfall.

Bolan carefully worked his way through the barrels toward the door. As he moved, he constantly reiterated and reevaluated his understanding of the situation. Such analytical skills had been the margin between life and death for Bolan many times in the past. The MPCI rebels had been driven out of their border refuges and deeper into the Burkina Faso interior by advancing Ivory Coast army forces. After being routed from the border stations they had fallen back into the Yendere township, among others.

It was unsurprising that their security formations inside the township were so inefficient as they were little more than a well-armed street gang. What Bolan found strange was the lack of evidence of Ivory Coast national forces, other than the craters left by artillery rounds. Had they stopped their advance once word of the mobilized Burkina military had reached them?

A burst of gunfire erupted from inside the garage. The sound of a Kalashnikov firing was unmistakable to Bolan. A flurry of rounds struck the wall along the second story of the hotel. Green tracers arced across the square. Bullet holes tore into the clay-brick structure already tattooed with the scars of weapon fire. A windowpane was shattered and glass tinkled.

He rose out of his crouch behind the oil barrels and began jogging across the short distance to the building's back door. The MAT-49 was up and held tight in his fists. A short burst of gunfire lashed out from the hotel and raked the side of the garage.

As the rounds struck the structure, Bolan ran and kicked the flimsy door off its moorings. The door imploded off its hinges, splintering under the impact of his boot tread. Leading with his MAT-49 submachine gun, Bolan burst into the building.

An old red Toyota hatchback was up on the racks above a mechanic pit. Its windows were gone, and its frame had been riddled and dimpled with machine-gun fire. Bolan ducked below the raised vehicle to get a better look inside the unlit garage bay.

He saw two men hunkered down behind the concrete walls on either side of a bullet-riddled service bay door. Spotting Bolan, they spun, bringing up AKM assault rifles as he burst in on them. Their expressions were almost comically startled. Bolan raked them both with 9 mm rounds from the French submachine gun, stitching a line of slugs across one rebel gunman's chest.

The racket of his firing was deafening in the confined space of the room. Shell casings spit out of the MAT-49's oversize ejection port and spilled across the floor. They bounced across the oil-stained concrete and rolled into the open mouth of the mechanic pit under the red Toyota. The muzzle on the MAT-49 climbed with the recoil of Bolan's continuous blasts, and the tail end of his burst buried four slugs in the second rebel fighter's head.

The gloom was so deep in the garage bay that each burst of automatic gunfire lit up the room like a strobe light, casting weird shadows across bullet-pocked walls and the dimpled metal body of the red Toyota.

The guerrilla's skull bounced crudely off the wall, leaving a smear of crimson clinging to it as he slid down. Bolan eased up on the trigger of the MAT-49 and turned the weapon back on the first rebel. Blood leaked out of the man's slack mouth and trickled down both sides of his chin.

Bolan fired a neat 3-round burst into him, then turned and repeated the procedure in the second man. A bottle half full of grain alcohol slid out of the dead man's hand and rattled on the floor. Liquor rushed out of the bottle and mixed with the growing pools of red. Free from the suppressive effect of the rain outside, the stink of burned cordite filled Bolan's nose. Smoke trailed up from the muzzle of the submachine gun, and Bolan shifted his gaze around the room.

Bullets suddenly poured through the wooden door leading into the side office of the garage. Bolan threw himself down and forward. He hit the ground hard and rolled forward to drop into the service pit. He landed in the little concrete hole on his feet. He raised the old French submachine gun above his head and fired a blind burst of suppressive fire as he moved toward the front edge of the work pit.

The little weapon shook and stuttered in his hands as he came up against the wall. Bullets from inside the garage office tore through the flimsy door and shot around the room, ringing off the Toyota's frame, hitting walls and whistling through blown-out windows.

Bolan's weapon jerked in his hand as the last round fired and the bolt snapped open. He tossed the submachine gun to the side and drew his Desert Eagle. He rested the big handgun on the oil-stained floor of the garage and trained the sights on the pockmarked office door. He knew there was an even chance the gunman on the other side of the door was so stoned that he'd rush through in an attempt to finish him off. There was also every chance the gunner was nowhere near that gutsy.

Bolan heard a voice shout something from across the street in the vicinity of the mosque. A higher pitched voice answered from inside the garage office. Bolan shifted his feet and looked around, trying to ascertain if any other rebel troops were in a position to direct the actions of the man in the office or to draw down on Bolan himself.

Outside the rain was falling with such force that the raindrops bounced when they hit the ground. Water flooded the narrow ditches beside the street and stood in a shallow lake across the square. Vision was obscured in the dark at ten yards, and everything beyond twenty was an indiscriminate blur. Only the flash of muzzle-fire would be visible from across the street.

Bolan watched the office door in the sudden lull. He tried to peer through the bullet holes to see into the room beyond, but the angle was wrong. He decided to fix that. He carefully aimed the .44 Magnum pistol. He tightened his grip and forced air in a steady stream out of his nose.

He squeezed the trigger.

The pistol roared in his hand and a muzzle-flash almost a foot long spilled from the massive barrel. The gun jerked back against his grip, and Bolan automatically adjusted for the recoil pressure. The big slug struck the ratty, bullet-riddled door in the flimsy lock mechanism and blew apart the handle.

A fist-sized hole appeared in the door, and the bullet snapped the latch cleanly. The kinetic force shoved the door open. It swung inward, and Bolan caught a glimpse of an ancient desk and a grimy vending machine. He saw the startled gunman was flattened on the floor.

The boy was maybe twelve, and the Chinese Type 56 assault rifle he was trying to aim looked ridiculously large against his slight, bony frame. Bolan knew child-soldiers were a fact of life in Africa. The warlords took them as young as eight, hooked them on narcotics and gave them weapons. They often proved to be the most brutal, most merciless of killers.

The boy looked at Bolan from where he was stretched out, his eyes as big as saucers. Bolan was disgusted. He would not kill a child.

The big American shifted the Desert Eagle away from the boy and fired into the office. The bullet struck a tattered office chair in the backrest, tearing through the chair and sending it tumbling across the room, spinning out of control. The Executioner shifted and fired the big gun again. A hole the size of a fifty-cent piece ripped open in the side of the vending machine, and the sound of the impact was like a baseball bat on a countertop.

The boy shrieked in terror and dropped his weapon. Scrambling frantically to his feet, the boy dived toward the office door and out into the rain. Bolan worked his jaw grimly, attempting to pop his ears from the ringing gunfire.

He slid down behind the protective cover of the mechanic pit to avoid any return fire from outside the building. He holstered the Desert Eagle and took the Simonov SKS carbine from the sling around his body. He ejected the 10-round magazine of 7.62 mm bullets, looked at the count and shoved it back home.

He thought about securing one of the AKMs from the rebels he'd shot, then decided against risking the potential exposure. He wrapped the slack from the rifle sling around one arm and crawled up out of the mechanic pit.

The killing had only just begun.

14

Bolan slid up to the broken back door of the garage and peered cautiously out into the rain. He left the incident in the mechanic garage behind him. He'd known from the beginning he'd have to shoot his way in and shoot his way out. He compartmentalized the desperate combat and put it away. It entered into his memory alongside other, older memories and it stayed there. It was his gift, an ability that few shared and that allowed him to continue on after the most horrific violence. For Bolan, the moment things were done, they were done.

The rain did not give up its secrets easily. Bolan knew it only made sense that, if the MPCI rebels wanted to take whoever was holed up inside the hotel, they would surround the building from all sides.

But the rebels were unprofessional, lacked good communications and were uncoordinated. A great portion of them were stoned most of the time, and the others were drunk. The rains had greatly hampered the ability of the Burkina motorized forces to maneuver the only road into the town, and the same rain had prevented the artillery pieces of the Ivory Coast national army from being decisive because the soldiers fired on line of sight and not through the use of trained forward observers. In the heavy rain their superior firepower was lost because targets were invisible.

Despite this Bolan knew the town had to be crawling with MPCI rebels, stoned, psychotic child-soldiers more at home terrifying civilian populations than in professionally executed military operations. Bolan might have been able to infiltrate in and out under their noses if not for the boy. He hadn't been able to bring himself to kill him, and now his operational security was probably blown.

It would be moments before the boy spread the word, if he hadn't already. Once the guerrilla forces learned the story of a lone white man fighting independent of Ivory Coast or Burkina forces the situation would change drastically. Bolan knew he'd become the focal point of their activities.

The Executioner gazed along the rooftops, then doorways and second-story windows. The buildings directly behind the Kibidwe Hotel were open air under thatched roofs with livestock pens placed behind some of them.

A huge pile of raw, white cotton was heaped loosely like hay under a tin roof. Bolan crouched, holding the SKS at port arms and slid through the open door. He took up position among the oil barrels lined up on the opposite side of the door frame from the direction he'd approached the garage.

A rebel sniper in the market strolled around a thick center pillar. His rifle, a battered old SVD 7.62 mm Dragunov sniper rifle was fitted with a PSO-1 telescopic sight offering a 4-power magnification. The man was dressed in French Foreign Legion camouflage he'd scrounged somewhere and held his rifle ready.

The gunman was reacting to the gunfire he'd heard from inside the garage. Bolan leveled his SKS across the top of an oil barrel, quickly lowered the rear sites to the factory setting and set his point of aim. The range was right at fifty yards and over such a short distance the high-caliber round was bound to rise only slightly, if at all.

As he watched the man searching for a target, Bolan took a quick check of the area around the man to make sure he was alone. He nestled the rifle buttstock into his shoulder and got a good weld with his cheek as he settled into a comfortable firing position.

It would be a clean shot, Bolan knew. The rebel sniper looked over toward the back of the Kibidwe Hotel, then back toward Bolan's position. Without warning the man began shooting indiscriminately in Bolan's direction.

Bolan squeezed the trigger.

The rifle recoiled smoothly into his shoulder, but the Executioner knew as soon as he had pulled the trigger that his shot was off. The wood of the pillar to the right of the gunman's head exploded as the round struck.

Bolan snarled. The front sight had been dinged at some point, either by him or by its original owner. The rebel gunman sprang back, surprised by the return gunfire. He squatted, looking instinctively toward the hotel to see where the shot had come from.

Rising, Bolan tried to compensate for the damaged sight by using Kentucky windage. He pulled the trigger again, catching the sniper in profile. The 7.62 mm round struck the man high in the left shoulder.

The rebel was driven up hard against a pillar and spun halfway around. Blood blossomed and instantly stained his uniform scarlet. Face a stricken mask, the rebel looked out into the rain from his position under the roof and realized just how exposed he was.

Bolan squeezed the trigger on the SKS again as the man threw himself to the ground. The shot tore through the open air where the man had been standing. Bolan gritted his teeth. From that angle he could no longer fire on the man and remain within the protection of the oil barrels. He moved forward, triggering the SKS again and again in semiautomatic blasts of rifle fire. The wounded rebel saw the muzzle-flashes and tried to pick up the long barreled Dragunov and bring it to bear. Bolan pulled the trigger on his SKS three times, striking the rebel once in the hip and once in the lower back.

The MPCI rebel spasmed like a fish pulled into the bottom of a boat, then lay still, his eyes wide open and blindly staring. Blood began to quickly pool around his lax body, and it flowed straight toward the pile of raw cotton, staining it bright red along the bottom.

Bolan had enough of the SKS. He threw down the weapon and drew his Beretta 93-R machine pistol. He continued out from behind the tangle of oil barrels and trotted into the alley. He was only a few short yards from the hotel's back door.

Two MPCI rebels came jogging out of the downpour. They held their weapons up and ready but seemed more curious than aware that they were walking into potential danger. Without conscious thought, Bolan dropped to one knee in the middle of the alley, brought up the Beretta in a two-fisted grip and dropped the men from twenty yards. They dropped to the ground like wet sacks of cement. Bolan began moving quickly toward the men. One of them had been armed with a more modern AKS-74 with a folding stock, and Bolan intended to make it his own.

The Executioner reached the dead men and bent down. His hand grasped the assault rifle and he pulled it out of the slack grip of the dead guerrilla. Holstering his Beretta, he held the rifle up to inspect it.

As abruptly and suddenly as if someone had flipped a switch, the rain stopped. The monotonous downpour evaporated. Bolan blinked, looking around. He'd known such changes were common in the rainy season, but actually experiencing it was an uncanny feeling.

He realized he was suddenly exposed to any number of gunmen to whom only moments before he had been invisible. He turned and rushed toward the rear entrance of the hotel.

He heard someone shout, then another voice joined in. He covered the muddy ground like a sprinter, running hard with the AKS-74 up and at the ready. He looked up and saw the rear of the hotel clearly. The building's surface was pockmarked with bullet holes, and not a single window remained unbroken.

He scanned the building, looking for the door. It had been shot a dozen times but still held on by its hinges and latch. He put his head down like a running back breaking through a defensive line and charged the doorway. A second before he struck the door he jumped and aimed both feet at it.

He heard a burst of machine-gun fire from behind him as he hit the door. There was a pop and the sound of wood splintering as he crashed through the structure. His foot tangled up with the damaged wood and he fell heavily on his side astride the broken door. Bolan hissed in pain as his already bruised and abused body absorbed more blunt trauma. He pushed himself up and scooted to the side, away from the opening. Bullets, like angry hornets, buzzed through the gaping doorway and slapped into the walls.

As Bolan rose, he saw that he was in a small, narrow room. There were garbage cans lined up against the wall and several old buckets on wheels. Black rubber boots were arranged against one wall, and greasy aprons hung from metal hooks.

"Saragossa," Bolan called out as he stood.

There was no answer but Bolan remained tensed. The MPCI gunmen were rabble, but they should have been able to take the hotel if they'd wanted. A determined gunman could hold out against fighters of their caliber for a long time, but the hotel was simply indefensible for a single person. There were too many approaches, too many entrances, too many angles of fire.

Despite that, the rebels hadn't entered the hotel but instead had held themselves back to only surrounding the building. Bolan frowned as he began to move. The guerrillas had surrounded the hotel and then took up *defensive* positions, performing holding actions. Was it possible they had been containing Saragossa in the building instead of trying to drag her out?

Bolan brought up the AKS. He looked over his shoulder at the open door. The room was black, and the gloom from outside was a bar of lighter gray in comparison to the cavelike dark of the little antechamber. Bolan squinted and turned back toward a pair of swing doors.

A machine gun opened up, and a flotilla of bullets sailed in through the outside door. The rounds struck the mops and tore into the garbage cans, scattering them across the floor. Gouges of wood paneling were ripped out of the wall, and coat hooks were torn off their housings.

Bolan pushed through the swing doors and entered a large kitchen with a long metal table running the length of the room between sets of ovens and outdated microwaves. Pots and pans hung from racks overhead, and the shelf under the food preparation table contained more of the same. Across the room a second set of swing doors hung still, leading deeper into the hotel. Bolan took a pair of quick steps and leaped up onto the metal table, sliding across it and landing on the other side.

He had no intention of trying to hold off the gunmen if they chose to assault the building. It was a hopeless task, and he would only become bogged down. Speed of movement and aggression were the only things that could save him now.

"Saragossa!" he bellowed.

He pushed his way through the kitchen swing doors. The dining room ran from the food preparation area out to about three-quarters of the way toward the front wall of the hotel and was filled with tables and chairs of dark wood. The last part of the big room was taken up by an empty fireplace, and several comfortable chairs forming a sitting area in front of two huge picture windows that had been blown into jagged slivers.

Through the shattered glass Bolan could clearly see the wall running around the mosque directly across the township square. Two men jogged out the front gate, one holding an RPK machine gun and the other a battered, green ammo box. They headed quickly toward the government offices on the other end of the square. Bolan chose to ignore them for the moment.

He turned and looked across the low wooden wall that served as a divider between the restaurant and lounge areas and the front desk. The counter behind which the clerk would have stood was also of dark wood, and the entire building reeked of French influence. Beside the front desk and opposite from the front doors was a narrow staircase, which led to the second floor.

"Saragossa!" Bolan called out, keeping his voice lower this time.

He crossed out of the dining room through an opening in the dividing wall and into the front lobby area. He checked over his shoulder to make sure rebel gunmen hadn't rushed into the kitchen behind him. There was no sign of movement.

He took a couple of tentative steps toward the stairs, AKS

at the ready. He looked over his shoulder and back out the front window and saw the machine-gun crew had halted before reaching the government offices. In the lee of a shot-to-hell Citroën pickup truck they had set up a hasty fighting position, the RPK sat on its bipod with the muzzle trained on the front of the hotel.

Bolan moved quickly to the foot of the stairs and stopped. A rebel lay sprawled head down on the first couple of steps. His left eye and part of his forehead had been blown away at such close range that Bolan could see the powder burns. The gunman's blood covered the floor.

"Saragossa! Are you up there?" he called out.

Bolan wouldn't enter the killzone of the stairs, despite the pressing matter of time. It was too reckless, too needlessly suicidal. He crouched beside the front desk, holding the AKS muzzle up. He constantly shifted his gaze from the kitchen doors to the front of the hotel and then back to the stairs.

From the front of the building Bolan heard an excited shouting break out from the gate of the mosque. One of the machine gunners shouted back at the men behind the wall and Bolan knew what was coming even though he didn't understand the language.

The RPK opened up. Green tracer fire poured through the front window and smashed into the dining room of the hotel. Rounds struck tables and splintered chairs. Bullets clawed into the faded wallpaper and knocked pictures off the walls. Bullets blew chunks of mortar off the fireplace mantel and punched through sofas and chairs, sending stuffing billowing into the air.

Bolan popped up and set his elbows on the top of the bell desk. He centered his rear and front sights, puffed out a breath and squeezed the trigger. The bolt cycled once and tossed the spent shell onto the floor. Out in the courtyard the machine gun trigger man slumped dead, a chunk of his forehead jutting out from his skull at a rude angle. The assistant gunner shrieked and leaped to his feet. He spun, slipping in the mud, and tried to scramble for the protection of the Citroën truck. Bolan put a single round through his neck and sent him tumbling to the muddy ground.

Screams and shouts erupted from the rebel fighting positions in the mosque and government office building. Arcs of automatic weapon fire streamed from the two locations, converged and began striking the front of the hotel.

Bolan spun and moved to the stairs. Bullets blasted into the lobby behind him. He stuck his head around the corner of the hotel stairs and then ducked back quickly. He had seen nothing.

"Saragossa, I'm coming up!" he shouted.

Bolan gritted his teeth when he got no response and forced himself to turn the blind corner. He had come far and suffered much in the short time he had been in-country. He had to turn the corner and he knew it. Saragossa was still the one holding all the cards.

He held his AKS to the ready but down as he slid around the corner and onto the stairs. He moved slowly, eyes peering up into the murky stretch of the staircase. He placed his feet carefully around the shot-up rebel corpse so as not to trip. The soles of his boots were thick with bloody mud and left messy footprints on the old wood.

Bolan took each step carefully, peering into the shadowed gloom. There was not the slightest hint of motion from the upper story. He knew if he was caught on these stairs he was dead. He could see the railing at the top of the staircase and caught a glimpse of the walls beyond it on the second-floor landing. He stepped up past the dead rebel soldier's feet and climbed a few more steps. The creaking of the old wood seemed ridiculously loud given the cacophony of automatic weapon fire that had just torn up the lobby. Bolan eased himself up another step.

He could see the tops of doorways breaking the line of the wall through the bullet-chewed banister around the landing. None of them stood open. Bolan went up several more steps and noticed the haze of gun smoke hanging in the thick, humid air.

His head cleared the landing and he stopped, taking everything in. There were eight rooms on the floor, each with its door shut. The walls showed scorch marks from tracer fire, and bullets pockmarked the flower and ivy pattern wallpaper. Next to the railing, a second rebel gunman lay facedown in his own blood. At the end of the landing a window set over the hotel's front doors had been blown out. A pile of loose shell casings lay under it, alongside empty magazines for what Bolan thought might be an Uzi submachine gun.

Bolan climbed fully onto the landing. He nudged the body of the rebel at the top of the stairs, confirming he was dead. The confined hallway reeked of cordite and the fresh slaughtered stink of the dead rebel gunmen.

Bolan could hear voices coming in through the broken window. He backed out of the center of the hall and headed toward one side of the landing in case he was silhouetting himself to any shooters outside. He had exposed himself to ambush by Saragossa already, and he figured that if she had intended to kill him she would have already tried. If she was here at all, then she was behind one of those hotel-room doors.

"Saragossa," Bolan said softly. "Saragossa, I'm here to help you."

"I'm in here," she answered.

Bolan turned toward the door closest to the hall window. The voice had been a warm and rich alto, husky and thick. The pain was obvious though she controlled it well.

Bolan crossed to the door, hugging the wall. He knew what he was going to find even before he opened the door.

15

The Executioner turned the knob on the door and it unlatched.
He put his fingertips against the wood and gently pushed. It
swung open under his touch while Bolan kept himself poised.

"Don't shoot," he said in English. The phrase sounded
slightly ridiculous to his ears.

"Are you unarmed?" Saragossa asked, then laughed.

Grudgingly, Bolan felt the corners of his mouth tug up.
"Hell, no."

"Come in," she said.

Bolan lowered his weapon to his hip, holding the AKS-74
so that the muzzle was pointed down. He stepped out into the
bar of light directly in front of the open door. He could make
out a shape against the far wall of the small room. The single
bed had been overturned, as had the dresser.

Two MPCI rebels lay dead, sprawled across the middle of
the floor in a pool of red. The wall behind them had been splattered with their blood. Flies were thick in the room. They
stirred and lifted in a black cloud from the corpses in lazy
protest as Bolan entered.

The Executioner stepped into the room. Saragossa looked
up at him from the floor. There was a mini-Uzi machine pistol
in her lap, held loosely in her right hand. The mercenary

looked up at Bolan through heavily lidded eyes. Her left arm had swollen to such a point that her skin seemed almost ready to burst open.

"What happened?" Bolan asked.

"Scorpion."

"You have antivenin?"

"Yes, for snakes, for cobras. Both use neurotoxins in their venom."

"Can you move?" Bolan asked.

"Not really. Being stung slowed me down. I took a round in the gut through the window."

Bolan moved in closer and knelt beside Saragossa. "Let me see."

The woman let the hand holding the bloody cloth over her lower abdomen fall away. Blue-green flies buzzed around them. Bolan frowned but forced himself to suppress any outward reaction. He looked away from the glistening coil of Saragossa's intestine and out the window. Thick clouds were low and black in the sky.

"It's bad," he admitted.

"I don't suppose you have a medevac waiting?" Saragossa smiled. Her voice was a whisper and her skin was ashen.

"No, that wasn't part of the plan," Bolan said.

He stood and went to the overturned bed, grabbed a pillow from the floor and pulled off the case. He turned it inside out, then pulled out his knife and began cutting the bedsheets into strips.

Saragossa watched Bolan with dull, glassy eyes as he took her first-aid kit and added it to his assembled supplies. He went to the door and opened it wide, giving him a view into the hallway from where Saragossa was propped against the wall.

Moving back to Saragossa, he passed in front of the

window and looked at the mosque across the street from the hotel. Gunfire erupted from the structure and struck the wall outside. Bolan dropped quickly. Rounds from an assault rifle struck the hotel outside the window again. Several bullets including a green tracer round buzzed into the room.

"That was sloppy of me," Bolan muttered.

He squatted on his knees beside the gravely wounded woman. She looked up at him and tried to smile as he set his rifle on the floor.

"Don't tell me about sloppy," she slurred. "I'm the one with the bullet in me."

Bolan grunted and tried to smile. He picked up Saragossa's mini-Uzi, popped the magazine and checked how full it was. He reinserted the magazine into the pistol-grip well and carefully placed the weapon on Saragossa's leg below her wound.

He took a pair of white latex gloves out of her little field kit and pulled them on. He knew it was probably a losing battle to try to keep the wound clean in this kind of environment, but he was going to at least make the effort.

"This is going to hurt," he warned.

Saragossa closed her eyes and nodded briefly. A stream of automatic fire burst through the window above their heads and hammered into the room. Bullets hurtled into the open door and rattled it on its frame. Bolan ignored the fire but shot a look toward the now fully ruined door to the room. The hall outside remained empty.

With his thumb Bolan spun the cap on top of the little travel bottle of hydrogen peroxide. The cap came loose and shot across the room, bouncing off the dresser and hitting the floor. He didn't warn Saragossa again but instead simply upended the bottle and poured the disinfectant over her wound.

Saragossa gasped at the sudden shock. Her eyes shot open

wide and she made as if to sit up, but Bolan put a gentle hand on her shoulder, easing her back down. The hydrogen peroxide bubbled and became a white froth over the area of exposed flesh. It made a sound almost like a sizzle.

Bolan waited for Saragossa to regain her composure.

"Is there an exit wound?" Bolan asked.

The woman shook her head. "Where's the rest of your team?" she suddenly asked.

"We had an unexpected meeting with Burkina customs. I went ahead while the group deals with that," Bolan lied.

"You couldn't buy your way out of trouble?"

"They're jumpy right now, because of the MPCI and the Ivory Coast nationals."

Bolan waved his hand and shooed flies away before taking the small quantity of gauze dressings Saragossa had and placing them across the wound, where they stuck and immediately turned red. He gave the hall outside another quick check when he was finished.

The big American saw the top of a head breach the lip of the stairs followed almost instantly by a pair of dark eyes. Bolan picked up the mini-Uzi and straightened his arm out as the man struggled to bring up an old Soviet AKM in the narrow confines of the staircase and twist it over the edge to fire on Bolan.

The Executioner pulled the trigger on the mini-Uzi machine pistol. The gun snarled and 9 mm bullets dug up gouges out of the hall floor as Bolan walked his burst onto target. The MPCI soldier's right elbow came up sharply behind his head as he tried to pull the AKM back, then shove it forward and return fire through the railing struts. Splinters of wood tore off and spun through the air.

The first of two bullets struck the man in the crown of his

head and knocked him back. A red cloud of bloody spray haloed the man's skull, then he dropped out of sight. Bolan waited, machine pistol poised. He had to move Saragossa, but if he moved her before he bandaged her, then she would never survive. If he moved her out of the line of fire while he tried to bandage her, then he would be unable to cover the egress point the stairway provided the enemy.

There was no sign of movement in the stairway.

Bolan put the machine pistol down again and placed the folded pillowcase he had taken off Saragossa's bed over the bloody gauze bandages. He turned and picked up a length of sheet he'd cut into strips. He heard something on the stair and picked up the Uzi and fired a burst through the door opening. His rounds tore into the wooden railing of the banister, chipping wood and snapping support struts.

He quickly set the machine pistol down and encouraged Saragossa to lean forward which she did, moaning with the pain. He looped the ends of the cloth strip around her torso and then helped her lean back.

"They're coming," he whispered tersely. "Tie those sheet ends into place the best you can."

The knee of Bolan's pants had become stiff with dried mud but kneeling in Saragossa's blood moistened the material again and it clung to his skin with a warm, slimy sensation as he rose in a combat crouch. Keeping away from the window and watching the hall, Bolan picked up his AKS-74 and ducked under the sling so that it hung off his shoulder and down across his body with the pistol grip dangling by his right hip. Once he had situated the folding stock carbine Bolan took up the Uzi machine pistol in a two-fisted grip.

He eyed the staircase and had no illusions. The woman was unstable and couldn't be moved. He had no place to move her to or any means of transportation anyway. The freelance operative was going to die in this stinking hotel room.

His mind raced, and cold logic fought with emotion and his own sense of a warrior's ethics. The information she had was vital to the U.S. government and the people of the world. Bolan believed this with true conviction and without question. Marie Saragossa had to give up her information. He waved a few fat flies away from his face.

"If we can hold out long enough, I believe my team will arrive shortly," Bolan said.

"Good," Saragossa whispered. Her voice sounded wet, it almost gurgled.

"But you know why I'm here. I need you to tell me what you found and where it is."

"Business first?" She tried to laugh.

Bolan heard the pain in her voice and risked a look at the woman. A stray round shot into the room. He barely flinched. Saragossa looked ghastly. She shifted her head and fixed him with a stare. Her eyes were glassy.

"Who are you?" she asked.

Bolan froze for a moment, then glanced away from the dying woman and back toward the open door.

"Now that your dressing is in place we should move you out of view of the door," Bolan said.

"No," Saragossa said.

"What do you mean 'no'?"

"I'm afraid the scorpion will get me again." Her voice sounded far away.

"The scorpion's still in here?" Bolan asked.

"Under the bed, I think."

"I won't let anything happen to you, I promise," Bolan lied. She smiled up at him, and the Executioner realized he didn't want this woman to die. But it didn't matter what he wanted, and he knew that. He looked back toward the stair landing, almost willing an MPCI guerrilla to appear so that he could exert his frustration in violent action.

He had seen Saragossa's wound up close. Bolan was no physician, but he had a lifetime of experience with bullet wounds. She had taken the round low, and the intestines had been damaged. The intestine carried biological impurities out of the body. The round had spilled that dirty matter into her blood and healthy tissue. The medical term was sepsis, and it meant that death was guaranteed without massive medical intervention. But it would be slow and painful.

"Who are you?" Saragossa asked again.

Her voice was weak, and the pain ran through it in a dark current. Bolan wasn't an espionage agent; lying was not part of his job description. He was a soldier and he saw things through a soldier's eyes. She lay there suffering with no hope of salvation or relief, yet he witnessed her strength and courage. And he had to lie to get what he needed.

"Who are you?" Saragossa repeated.

Her words were so weak they sounded like a sigh in Bolan's ears.

"My name is du Toit," Bolan said. "I don't know who spent the money, but I was sent to get you, or what you know."

"You're a mercenary?"

Bolan looked away from the dying woman and back to the hallway.

"There is no time. You were hired to find something out. You found it out. You need to tell me what it was."

"Am I going to die?" she asked.

Bolan was stunned by the naked strength of the acceptance in her voice. He looked straight into her eyes. "Yes," he said.

Too late he caught the flash of movement and spun on reflexes so honed by experience that they were nearly preternatural. The mini-Uzi burped as he pulled the trigger. From the stairs the man charged upward, a Chinese Type 56 assault rifle screaming staccato shrieks in his hands.

The rounds, 7.62 mm Warsaw Pact ball ammunition, forked out from the muzzle. Rounds poured into the hotel room as the man cleared the landing edge and bounded onto the second floor of the hotel.

Bolan shifted naturally, like a dancer responding to a cue, his own weapon firing in response. The assault rifle's burst clawed up the floor, chewing through it as the stream of fire bore straight down onto Bolan. The Executioner tightened his own burst and put it on target and directly into his attacker. The MPCI guerrilla soaked up the rounds and stopped short at their impact.

A volley of 9 mm rounds tore into the Chinese assault rifle, smashing the wooden grips and frame before ricocheting off the metal barrel and receiver in a spray of sparks. Other rounds punctured the guerrilla's limbs, and geysers of blood spouted as the bones of the man's forearms were shattered under the impact of the high-velocity rounds.

Bolan let the muzzle climb as he kept the trigger down. Three rounds arced over the assault rifle and slammed into the skinny man's chest, smashing bones and ripping into muscles.

The guerrilla shook with the impact of Bolan's rounds. His assault rifle fell to the floor and the man collapsed inward on himself like a house of cards folding under a careless hand. Bolan saw the man's mouth work as he tried to speak around the spilling blood, then his eyes rolled up, showing the whites and he plunged to the floor.

Bolan threw down the mini-Uzi, sure that its magazine

was spent. He dropped his right hand to his hip and claimed the pistol grip of his AKS-74. He raised it as his left hand dropped to find a handhold on the front stock.

He pushed the weapon out to the edge of its strap to steady it and squared his shoulder against the pull. His finger found the smooth metal curve of the trigger, and he swept the muzzle toward the stairs, tensed.

Nothing moved.

Bolan blinked the sweat out of his eyes and looked again. Nothing moved. The guerrilla Bolan had just stopped coughed wetly, then sighed with a sound like air escaping from a tire. Reassured that the attack was over for the moment, Bolan risked a glance back toward Saragossa.

More than one of the bullets from the gunman had caught her in the legs. Bolan saw a bullet wound in her thigh and saw another in her shin where the white fragments of her crushed bones showed up in vivid relief against the pink of her torn flesh and the scarlet of her spilling blood.

Bolan looked up at Saragossa's face. It was as white as chalk.

He realized she was so far gone she hadn't cried out at the impact of the new wounds.

"Marie," he said. "Tell me. What did you learn?"

She lifted her hand and pointed weakly toward the bed. She opened her mouth to speak, and Bolan realized she was so weak he couldn't hear her. He shifted closer and bent down until his ear was almost touching the bloody swell of her lips.

"What?" he asked.

"My cell phone," she said. "I wrote it down, then took a picture with my cell phone. The grid coordinates and a summary of the record files. Short, but it will…tell you."

Her voice trailed off, and Bolan sat up and looked down at her. She looked back up at him and he watched her eyes become fixed. Just as suddenly her eyes relaxed. Bolan saw the light fade from them and the chalky gray of her skin spread to the beautiful brown of her irises and he knew she was gone.

Bolan reached out a hand and touched his fingertips to her eyelids, closing them. He looked up at the doorway, then back down at the dead woman's face.

Outside the window he heard the sound of vehicle engines running, then car doors slamming. There was a rush of orders given in French with an Afrikaans accent.

Bolan knew du Toit had arrived.

16

Bolan moved quickly to the bed where Saragossa's backpack lay open with its contents spread around in a pile on the overturned mattress. He shifted his hand through the clothes and personal items, hunting for Saragossa's cell phone.

He caught a flicker of motion out of the corner of his eye and looked down. Am amber-bodied scorpion scuttled out from under the bed. Bolan lifted his muddy boot and stomped on the creature. He heard the exoskeleton crack.

The warrior turned and began hunting through Saragossa's effects until he found the cell phone. Outside he heard more shouted orders. Another burst of fire entered the room through the window, and Bolan sank to one knee as he opened the phone.

He worked the buttons on the control pad furiously, looking up to the open door every few seconds. It would be no good for him to escape the hotel room only to find Saragossa had kept more than one cell phone. He needed to verify he possessed her information before he began his run.

He opened the menu and went to the camera option. He tapped his thumb against the button and scrolled down through a multitude of touristy pictures obviously designed as cover. Then he found the photograph of a yellow legal page of handwritten notes sandwiched between a picture of the mosque across the street and two smiling boys using acacia tree branches as switches to drive sheep.

Satisfied, Bolan snapped the phone shut and secured it in a pocket. He took up his Kalashnikov and started for the door to the room. Outside the broken window he heard what sounded like thunder in the distance. He knew it wasn't thunder. It had to be 82 mm mortar rounds. With the break in the rain the Ivory Coast nationals had begun their assault again. It would take only a few such weapons to level the entire town.

Bolan moved into the hallway, held up the Kalashnikov and looked down the staircase as he reached the landing. He saw only corpses on the stair but heard movement from the lobby below. He triggered a burst of harassing fire downward to temper any enthusiasm on the guerrillas' part.

Pulling his weapon back, Bolan began to move at quick time toward the end of the second story hallway. Outside he heard a shell detonate somewhere close to the township. He knew there would be a hell of a lot more fire after the artillery spotters noted where the reconnaissance rounds landed.

Bolan shouldered through the last door at the end of the hallway. The room was empty and identical to Saragossa's, only the single window overlooked the alley Bolan had used to approach the hotel. He let the Kalashnikov hang from its strap and used both hands to slam open the still intact window.

He stepped back from the sill and moved to one side. He pressed up against the wall next to the window frame and looked out over the rooftops and alley in one direction. Seeing nothing, Bolan maneuvered to the opposite side and repeated the process. He could see nothing, which only meant troops weren't standing in the open or moving through his field of vision.

Two shells struck the township and exploded. Bolan couldn't see where they impacted. From in the hall he heard machine-gun fire coming from downstairs as the troops below prepared to assault the second floor.

Bolan made his decision.

He sat on the window ledge and swung his legs through the opening. Taking the Kalashnikov in his right hand and grasping the bottom of the sill with his left, Bolan bounced himself off the lip and pushed away from the wall with his left hand.

He dropped two stories like a stone, striking the muddy ground with his feet together and his knees bent to absorb the force of landing. As soon as the soles of his boots struck the soft muck of the alley, Bolan rolled down along his side, transferring the force of the impact along the length of his body the way he had been taught what seemed a thousand years ago. He was grateful for the rain that had made the ground so soft.

He rolled over his shoulder and came up on one knee, bringing the Kalashnikov to bear. His body, already bruised and stiff from the hard parachute landing and buffalo attack, screamed in protest, but no one attacked Bolan from that direction.

Bolan spun in a tight circle and scanned the opposite area. He saw nothing and leaped to his feet. He heard artillery shells detonating behind him, on the other side of the hotel, and crossed the alley, skirting the thatched roof stall where he had killed the MPCI armed with the Dragunov sniper rifle.

He ducked under the cover of the tin roof and heard more automatic weapons fire coming from inside the hotel. He heard a shout in what sounded like Dutch and knew the South African mercenaries were behind him. He risked a glance as he rolled over the rails and into the sheep pen behind the stall.

Two white men, one armed with a Remington 870 pump-action shotgun and the other with an H&K MP-5, were in the mouth of the narrow alley that ran between the hotel and the mechanic garage Bolan had cleared earlier. They wore U.S. Army "chocolate chip" style desert camouflage BDUs and boonie hats. Both men were tanned dark and wore thick beards. The man with the MP-5 was shouting something down the alley toward the main square while the one handling the Remington leveled it toward Bolan.

The Executioner flopped to the ground on his belly as 12-gauge shot tore into the wooden split rails of the sheep pen. The stink of sheep manure made soupy by the rains rankled his nose. He lifted the AKS-74 with one hand and leveled the barrel across the lowest rung of the fence. He triggered a wild burst and scattered the two men, sending them scrambling for cover.

Bolan jumped to his feet and took the Kalashnikov assault rifle in both hands before firing a second burst from the hip. The man with the MP-5 dived for cover behind the same oil barrels Bolan had used earlier. The other man threw himself down on the ground, hugging the side of the hotel wall in the narrow alleyway.

Bolan lifted the AKS-74 to shoulder level and began to dance backward as he fired. Beyond the two men he saw movement at the public square end of the alley. He blinked in surprise but continued firing. He saw the girl from Le Crème's den and the Banfora airport walking toward the mouth of the alley. There was a Land Rover with Burkina gendarme markings parked directly behind her.

The girl walked into the alley. She seemed in no hurry and didn't appear to notice the explosions, screams or gunfire all around her. She seemed in a daze, and across the distance Bolan could feel her eyes lock on to him with a jolt of electricity.

Du Toit rushed around the front of the gendarme vehicle. He had picked up a 7.62 mm AK-104 assault rifle with a shortened barrel, since the airport. He was yelling something, and Bolan realized with a start that instead of giving his men orders the mercenary was shouting at the girl.

The man behind the oil barrels popped up and sprayed the stall with his MP-5. Bolan ducked and sprinted across the sheep pen to the far side. He dived over the fence and stayed down when he hit the ground. Cradling the Kalashnikov carbine in the crook of his arms, Bolan crawled away from the animal pen toward a round silo used to store crops.

More high-explosive rounds began to fall. This time they hit much closer to the center of the township. Bolan knew the cluster of buildings around the main square would be a priority target for the mortar crews, which was part of the reason he was trying to made it back out to the edge of the township before deciding on how best to proceed with exfiltration. Two streets over from his position a shanty exploded when an artillery shell detonated after punching through its thin roof.

A white Land Rover gunned up the narrow alley. Gendarmes armed with AKM assault rifles hung out the front and rear passenger windows. The vehicle slid to a stop in front of the wool shearing stall, and the two Burkina gendarmes opened fire.

Bolan rolled onto his back as rounds chewed through the humid, hot air above him. He brought his AKS to bear and fired back at the men. His rounds dented and pockmarked the vehicle's doors. The light-skinned doors dimpled and crumpled under the 7.62 mm rounds.

A man in the back seat screamed as he was struck through the door by the high-velocity, heavy-caliber rounds. His weapon dropped out of his hands and clattered to the ground as he fell back into the vehicle. Bolan pulled the muzzle of his weapon up toward his chin as he fired, directing his rounds toward the front of the vehicle.

The rounds climbed as he swept them to the side. Bullets burrowed into the front gendarme's shoulder and neck after shattering the man's elbow. His rifle fell into the mud as well, and he slumped forward heavily. A torrent of blood spilled from the neck wound and rushed down the white door of the Land Rover as he spasmed.

Bolan rolled back onto his stomach. He pushed up with one hand and got to his knees, then rose to a crouch and scrambled toward the hard cover of the grain silo.

He heard men scream behind him, then their voices were drowned out by the shriek of an incoming mortar round. Bolan reached the curved wall of the mud hut silo and skirted around it. The 82 mm shell struck the empty sheep pen and detonated. Bolan felt the concussion slam into his back as he slid around the edge of the building. He heard shrapnel strike the silo in a steel rain, and his ears rang from the blast. The mortar crews had found their range now, he knew. One or two clicks on the sighting mechanism and the shells would begin dropping down on the mosque, hotel and center of town.

He thought of Saragossa lying dead in the hotel room, flies driven indoors by the rain feasting on her remains, crawling in a thick, black carpet across her once beautiful face. He hoped a mortar round blew the room to hell and gave the woman a burial by fire.

He thought about Le Crème's or du Toit's teenage mistress. He hoped du Toit would get her to cover. Bolan risked a look around the edge of the silo and saw the South African mercenary with the Remington running to the rail of the sheep pen. Miraculously the side of the fence was still intact.

The man took up a defensive position on one knee and lifted the pump-action shotgun to his shoulder. He scanned through the smoke and haze left by the mortar round, searching for Bolan. The muzzle of the sweeping shotgun froze as the man spotted Bolan peering around the corner of the silo, Kalashnikov up.

The South African's eyes widened in shock at seeing Bolan drawing down on him.

Bolan squeezed the trigger of the AKS-74, the bullet drilling the mercenary in the broad sweep of his jutting forehead. Bolan felt a flash of grim satisfaction as he saw the red mist explode from the back of the man's head in the familiar scarlet halo.

Bolan darted back around the side of the silo and began to run down the alley. Behind him he heard mortar rounds dropping into the square like bolts of thunder. He ran hard, cutting down dirt lanes and through filthy alleyways. He passed mud hovels and shanties built from corrugated pieces of sheet metal. He cut through hard-packed courtyards strung with clotheslines left bare in the rainy weather and chicken coops built right up against the sides of houses.

Several times he was forced to step over corpses prostrate in the mud as he ran. He turned a corner and saw a mongrel tearing at the limp arm of one such corpse. The dog lifted its bloody muzzle and snarled a warning at Bolan.

The Executioner came to a stop and faced the dog. The sight turned his stomach. He lowered the AKS and took it in his left hand. With his right hand he reached across and drew the silenced Beretta 93-R. The dog was too battle-hardened and knew what a gun was. It barked twice and then took off running.

Bolan holstered the pistol, took up the AKS and turned to

go. A vehicle drove out from the break between two rows of shanties. It was a white Toyota pickup truck with a machine gun mounted on a tripod in the back. Three guerrillas rode in the front compartment while two manned the weapon positioned in the rear flatbed.

The big American spun on his heel and darted back into the alley he had just emerged from. Behind him he heard men shouting and the sound of the Toyota's engine revving. A curt blast from the machine gun chased him as the driver gunned the engine.

Bolan turned left and knocked open the door to a little hovel. The vehicle turned the corner behind him, and the machine gunner spotted him entering the house. Immediately the guerrilla opened fire.

Bolan hit the dirt floor inside the hut. The 7.62 mm bullets made pinging sounds as they punched through tin sheets and buzzed into the house. Bolan rolled more deeply into the building as the wood of the front door disintegrated under the onslaught. Gray bars of light shot through holes left by the machine-gun fire and cut the gloom inside the hovel.

The impact of the rounds tore down the interior wall behind him and began to strike the floor as the machine gunner lowered his weapon, anticipating Bolan's movement to the floor to find cover.

Bullets tore into the building around him. The hovel was a single room with a hot plate for cooking positioned within reach of a filthy mattress. A cooking pan was knocked into the air and a dirty blanket torn to shreds as Bolan huddled against the relentless fire. Two windows facing the street and covered with grease paper were vaporized. Crater wounds exploded out of the mud brick and gritty material lifted a haze in the air.

Bolan waited for the gunfire to stop. Gouts of dirt spouted up like geysers from the blowholes of whales where rounds struck the earthen floor. The din was deafening.

Ejecting the magazine, Bolan slid his only fresh replacement into the well. He hit the slide release and chambered a round into the breech. He knew that for an assault to work, right before the guerrillas rushed the door, the machine gunner would cease firing. He tensed in preparation for the moment.

As he expected, the lull came.

Without hesitation Bolan lifted his weapon and sighted on the front door. The first rebel filled the frame, kicking the wooden shambles out of his way. The big American dropped him with a tight burst under the gunner's jaw. The man staggered back and collapsed in the threshold.

Bolan rolled and laid his rifle across the still warm corpse of the gunman. He had the impression of a second rebel coming toward the door from off to one side of the house, and he swiveled the AKS around and triggered a burst.

The Executioner's rounds tore into the man's thighs from point-blank range. The guerrilla was scythed to the ground, screaming. Bolan could see the Toyota parked directly in front of the house. The man in the back of the truck worked the slide and lowered his weapon's muzzle in response to Bolan's action.

The man shot in the legs lay within arm's reach, still screaming. The man clawed for the pistol grip of the AK-47 he'd dropped as he'd gone down. Bolan jammed the still smoking muzzle of his AKS into the man's face. The guerrilla choked on his own scream a heartbeat before the 5.45 mm hardball rounds blew a cavity into his head.

Even before he had finished firing, Bolan was rolling. As

he twisted over he saw the bodies strewed in the threshold shudder under the impact of the machine gun's rounds, splattering hot blood and chunks of flesh across the dirt floor and mud walls of the little hovel.

He kept rolling until he had passed under one of the room's two windows and up against the far interior wall. The vehicle outside was less than twenty yards away, and Bolan heard the machine gun jam.

Bolan didn't hesitate. He popped up like a demented jack-in-the-box and thrust the muzzle of his AKS-74 out the ruined remnants of the hovel's window. He saw the machine gunner open the feed cover on the machine gun and start yanking on the cocking handle, trying to clear a double feed. The driver opened the door of the Toyota pickup and lifted his AKM in an attempt to provide cover.

Bolan shot him first, splattering blood across the vehicle's dirty white exterior. He lifted the pressure on his trigger and shifted aim. As the machine gunner looked up at the blast that had killed his driver, Bolan put six rounds into his body and knocked him clear of the pickup bed.

For one long moment it was still and silent, then Bolan heard the mortar rounds dropping across the township. A frightened dog started barking. Time seemed to slow and stretch out with the peculiar elasticity specific to combat. Bolan pulled the muzzle of his AKS-74 back inside the window and lowered his rifle.

Outside the window the sky opened up without warning and the rains simply started pouring from the heavens like some biblical plague. The roar was significant, and the sudden release of atmospheric humidity was so strong Bolan was immediately aware of the white vapor his body heat made as it rose off him, like smoke lifting up from a fire.

Then his perception hit the fast-forward button and another guerrilla came through the door of the hovel with his assault rifle blazing.

17

Du Toit grabbed the girl and shoved her toward the entrance to the hotel. Exploding shells landed close by, and it seemed obvious the Ivory Coast mortar teams were walking their rounds directly into the township's mosque. The entire operation inside Yendere was a complete cluster-fuck circus, du Toit thought.

Le Crème had helped du Toit coordinate with the MPCI rebels on the issue of Saragossa, but almost as soon as the men had informed the South African of the woman holed up in the corner room of the Kibidwe Hotel, they had then reported the presence of another—a lone, white man who killed like a demon.

Infuriated, du Toit had deployed his men to encircle the building, then secure it. When the rains had let up, the mortar teams had begun their harassing fire. *Then* the son of a bitch had shot his way out of the hotel and the girl had started walking into the middle of a firefight as placid as a zombie.

Du Toit and the girl proceeded into the hotel. Le Crème had run into the building first, seeking shelter from the mortar rounds. When du Toit entered he found the Burkina colonel looking at a pile of corpses bunched up at the bottom of the stairs leading to the second level of the hotel.

The girl saw the bodies. "*Gunab.* Death follows *Gunab* like sunshine, it is how he built the rainbow," the girl said, referring to a popular West African folk story.

Le Crème seemed physically jolted by the girl's declaration. He spit something out in a tribal dialect du Toit couldn't follow. The South African looked from the excited gendarme colonel to the girl who had an almost smug expression on her face as she ignored Le Crème's energetic ramble.

Du Toit lifted his hand and swept it across the girl's face, the smack of the back of his hand popping like a gunshot. The girl staggered backward and blood poured freely from the corner of her mouth. She looked up at du Toit and gently lifted her hand to where her cheek was already bruising. She didn't make a sound.

"You pull something like that again," du Toit warned, "walking away from me, and I'll kill you where you stand. You aren't here to talk, so just keep your damn mouth shut."

One of du Toit's men, a burly redheaded mercenary named Johnston, entered the hotel lobby armed with an AK-104 followed by two black gendarmes carrying AKM assault rifles. Johnston looked at the girl and saw the blood on her mouth. He smirked.

"Take those two upstairs," du Toit ordered. "Search the room those idiot rebels were firing on, and see if Saragossa is still here."

DU TOIT LOOKED DOWN at Saragossa's body.

The muscles of the corpse had relaxed in death. It was too early for rigor mortis to have set in, and the skin had begun to sag and puddle into lax shapes. In addition to the mushy elasticity, the skin had started to display a grayish white tone on the top while the dark bruise color of liver mortis was already starting to show where blood had pooled in the lower portions of the body following the pull of gravity.

Flies crawled across her, and du Toit noticed that Saragossa's

left arm was swollen to almost twice the size of the right one.
Two red marks stood out prominently on the doughy flesh of
her hand.

"This is too bad? No?" Le Crème asked.

The gendarme colonel stood beside du Toit in the cramped
hotel room among the bloody corpses. For once du Toit was
grateful for the fat man's cigar. The stench of the smoke
helped keep the death stink from gagging the gathered people.

"Yes, since I was supposed to get her out of here, this *is*
too goddamn bad," du Toit replied.

From behind the two men the girl spoke.

"Where *Gunab* goes, death is."

"What the hell is she talking about with this *Gunab* crap?"
du Toit demanded.

Le Crème took his cigar out of his mouth and glared at the
girl with bloodshot eyes. He turned back to du Toit after a
moment.

"*Gunab* is nothing, a silly superstition, nothing more,"
he said.

"Like a spirit, a bloody ghost?" du Toit asked.

Le Crème nodded. "*Gunab* lived under a pile of rocks and
battled *Tsui-Goab,* the creator god. *Gunab* killed so many in
his battles that he became an emblem of death."

"And he built a rainbow? She said downstairs he made the
rainbow. How does a death spirit make a pretty rainbow?" du
Toit asked.

"He made it out of his dead enemies," Le Crème replied.
"It is a metaphor."

"Bloody sweet religion you got," du Toit said with a sneer.

"It is tribal superstition, nothing more."

A mortar round landed inside the walled courtyard of the
mosque. Du Toit frowned. He figured the hotel would be the

third target of opportunity for Ivory Coast forces, important only after the UNICEF offices and the mosque, but it had to be one of the major targets in Yendere. The little border town boasted a population of less than fifteen hundred. There simply weren't that many targets other than shanties and animal pens.

"What's wrong with her left hand?" du Toit asked.

"Looks like a snakebite, or possibly scorpion stings," Le Crème offered.

"She was poisoned *and* gut shot? Tough lady."

"Not tough enough," Le Crème pointed out.

"See if there is anything in her stuff that might be valuable," du Toit ordered Johnston. "Then we fall back onto the road out of the city and make contact with the home office in Pretoria."

"With the rain stopped the forces stationed in Niangoloko to the north should begin to move down into Yendere," Le Crème said.

"Is that going to be a problem?" du Toit asked.

"The army general will have authority here if that happens, not me."

"We in danger of being arrested?" du Toit demanded. The South African mercenary sensed he was being felt out for another bribe.

"Not as long as you are with me. But the troops won't help you and the MPCI guerrillas will be forced to evacuate the town. You won't be able to operate," Le Crème warned.

"I need to see how the home office wants to proceed."

He turned away from the colonel and addressed Johnston. "Meet me downstairs."

Du Toit grabbed the girl by her arm and pushed her rudely ahead of him and out of the room. The principals weren't going to be happy with the way things turned out, he realized. The operation had been a long shot anyway. What troubled him most was the role the mystery man had played.

He owed that man for the death of his men, soldiers sent on a rescue mission and brutally ambushed for their trouble. Those were the breaks in the mercenary game, but it still left a bitter taste in du Toit's mouth.

The real question, he reflected, was what the man's true objective had been. Had he come to kill Saragossa to prevent her from getting some information out, or had he come to get something she had? Du Toit figured the man his whore called the *Gunab* hadn't been sent to help Saragossa, since he'd ambushed du Toit himself, but had the man shot her? Had she been carrying something of value? Perhaps he'd know more when he talked to Pretoria.

It began to rain again.

18

Bolan threw himself to the side as he tried to bring his weapon around. He came up hard against the front inside wall of the hovel. He felt the sting of bullets as rounds clipped him in the shoulder, his forearm, the ribs and his waist. A bullet hit his canteen, splashing tepid water across his back and the room.

The bullets grazed him, skipping off his body in superficial wounds the way flat stones skipped across a lake. The skinny teenager behind the AK-47 screeched, his face twisted with murderous emotion as he fired wildly from the hip.

Bolan swung up the AKS and thrust the folding stock carbine out to the end of his extended arms. He pulled the trigger from a distance of less than twelve feet and saw his rounds hammer into the gunman's torso, snapping the youth's sternum in two.

The gunman gasped and staggered back. Bolan pulled the trigger again, knocking the MPCI triggerman farther back. The young killer hit the edge of the door and spun halfway around. His feet, clothed in filthy running shoes, tripped up on the corpse in the threshold and he fell.

Bolan rushed forward and pointed the muzzle of the AKS downward. He fired a short burst into the killer's head to finish him off, then snapped up the rifle to cover the doorway. Nothing happened. Outside, through the frame of the door, torrential rain poured down.

Bolan stepped up to the edge of the door and looked out. The Toyota pickup sat idling. Exhaust fumes poured from the tailpipe into the air. The rain had diluted the spilling blood in the bed of the pickup, and watery red washed over the lip of the missing tailgate and dribbled onto the ground. Bolan set his AKS-74 aside. He bent, picked up an AKM, then scavenged magazines from the corpses. He was thirsty but now had no water. The rain plastered his hair to his skull like a cap.

Jogging out into the rain, Bolan crossed the dirt yard to where the Toyota truck was parked. His bullets had shattered the driver's window of the open door. He looked inside the cab where the keys hung in the ignition. Bolan threw the AKM onto the passenger side of the seat and knocked some loose glass splinters onto the floor.

He slid in behind the wheel. The vehicle had an automatic transmission, and Bolan shifted it into drive. He checked his rearview mirror and could barely see anything through the driving rain. He figured that meant he would be just as difficult to see.

Bolan pulled away from the house and began driving down the narrow dirt alley. The Toyota sputtered a little as the transmission worked. He'd studied maps and satellite photos of Yendere in his hotel room in Banfora. He knew the rough layout of the town and, using the main highway out of town to the north and mosque as central points, he felt confident he could navigate it well enough despite not having memorized the streets, which was an impossibility given the ramshackle nature of the structures and alleyways.

Bolan knew he wanted to exit Yendere to the east. The southern and western portions of the township contained Ivory Coast national army positions, and the highway entering from the north held Burkina troops moving into place. To the east he would certainly run out of road, but it would allow him to escape the confines of the township quickly.

Bolan turned the Toyota around a corner and pulled onto the mouth of another dirt alley. A wide, unpaved avenue running east to west cut across the township through the houses in front of him. He stepped on the gas and turned the truck to the east. His windshield wipers worked furiously at full speed to keep up with the falling rain.

The rain came in through the broken driver's window and soaked him further. It kept his clothes wet, which was a blessing because the blood from his grazing wounds had begun to clot and the damp kept the fabric from being knotted up into the wound by coagulation. When he found a safe place he would treat the bullet grazes, but for now he had no time or medical supplies available. Bolan pulled the truck out into the center of the muddy street and accelerated as much as he felt was prudent under the conditions.

He passed through a four-way intersection moving fast. From off the adjoining street two pickup trucks pulled in behind Bolan and began to follow him. The first was a technical with a RPK machine gun mounted in the back. The gunner was wearing an olive-drab French army rain poncho with a hood. The second truck contained a squad of men wearing the same wet weather gear.

Bolan increased his speed.

Behind him a pickup truck increased its speed as well. The convoy stretched out as Bolan sped up and the other drivers copied him to catch up. The RPK gunner held his fire, though the muzzle of his weapon was leveled directly over the roof of the truck cab.

Bolan flicked his gaze to his rearview mirror. If they had made him, then why the hell weren't they opening fire? he wondered. Barely thirty yards separated his vehicle from the lead pickup truck. At that range the RPK would easily dismantle the thin-skinned Toyota Bolan drove.

Up ahead the street split around a building built up on the street. Bolan guided his truck to the left. Behind him the convoy rushed up to the forked intersection and at the last moment veered right.

Bolan sighed with relief.

Up ahead the road twisted in a lazy curve, and Bolan steered the Toyota through the first turn. He sat up and slammed on the brakes as he rounded the corner. Two ancient OD two-and-a-half-ton trucks sat parked nose to nose across the street, forming a roadblock.

Bolan slowed his Toyota as the gunmen controlling the checkpoint ran out of shanties on either side of the street waving at him to stop the truck. Bolan tapped his brakes hard, then smoothly threw his transmission into reverse and hit the gas pedal. Mud flew as his rear tires spun, digging for purchase. Finally they caught and his truck lurched backward.

He threw his arm across the back of the seat and twisted around to steer out his rear windshield as he gunned the pickup. A white man driving a technical with the corpse of a MPCI rebel in the back was hardly incognito.

So much for my quick getaway, Bolan thought. I might as well be a flashing neon sign. It had been a gamble for time, and the gamble hadn't paid off.

Bolan peered out his back window through the gray curtain of rain. He guided the truck back through the curve, hunting for a spot wide enough to allow him to perform a bootlegger maneuver and turn the nose of the truck around. He couldn't hear the guerrilla gunmen shouting over the rain, but he heard the clash of their automatic weapon fire as his windshield burst apart.

Glass shards sprayed Bolan's exposed neck and cheek, and rain lashed through the broken windshield. Instantly the cab was drenched with the torrential rainfall.

Steel-jacket rounds struck the seat, jolting it roughly under his arm. Bullets smashed into the cab's rear windshield, right in front of Bolan's face. He instinctively jerked his head away as the windshield cracked and spiderwebbed under the impact. Another round struck the damaged glass and punched a fist-sized hole through the rear window.

Bolan was driving blind. There was no way to guide the vehicle through such a downpour with a cracked or blown-out windshield. Rounds tore into the cab and through the vehicle's front grille. The frame reverberated with the impact of heavy-caliber bullets, shaking the steering wheel under his hand. It was only a matter of time before a bullet found his radiator, or his skull for that matter.

He whipped the wheel hard to the side, sliding the truck around until it was perpendicular to the road. Bullets struck along the length of the truck as Bolan threw open the door and dropped to the ground. He jumped back up and grabbed the AKM off the seat, dragging it to him. He rolled under the door and came up behind the front tire with the Toyota's engine block between him and the firing gunmen.

He looked across the street and saw a big building of some sort, made out of concrete blocks. The door had been ripped off its frame for an unknown reason and the entrance was an open, black mouth. Bolan coiled his legs under him as more automatic weapon fire rocked the truck. A bullet struck the radiator, and it began to hiss madly as compressed steam billowed out.

Bolan exploded upward and sprinted for the side of the road. Five steps into his run he stretched out like a great cat and dived forward. He cut through the falling rain like a six-foot missile. He saw the muddy earth rushing up to meet him, and he struck the ground with his rifle. He folded along one arm and rolled over his shoulder.

Completing the somersault, Bolan rose out of the crouch and threw himself toward the concrete steps leading up to the open door. Bullets tore chunks out of the steps as he scrambled up them. Bolan's face was a mask of blood from shattering glass and now the exploding concrete. The rain lashed into him, wiping him clean only for his chalky flesh to begin bleeding in incessant rivulets all over again.

His foot caught on the top step and Bolan sprawled out across the threshold, landing belly down. He grunted with the impact, then dug in with elbows and knees to scramble inside the doorway. Bullets struck the walls around him as he crawled into the building. He blessed the rain as he entered the sanctuary, then promptly rolled to his right out of the line of fire.

He quickly took stock of his surroundings. The interior of the building had been gutted sometime ago from the look of it. The room was twenty yards by about twenty yards of empty concrete floor. Oil stains marred the ground every few feet, and dust lay thick everywhere.

Bullets struck the front of the building outside as Bolan stood. The front wall of the building had no windows and ran unbroken except for the front door. He had no idea what the place had been designed or used for. Off to his left he saw a door and, other than that, the entire first floor of the structure was wide open and empty.

Bolan caught a whiff of something ugly and turned his head. He saw a pile of moldy fur and realized a dog had been killed in here. Ants swarmed over the decomposing carcass in a black frenzy. Bolan turned away. He saw several candles set in some bizarre pattern laid out toward the middle of the bay. The wax had melted and run down the candles, sticking them to the floor. Unsure what it was that he was seeing, Bolan dismissed it.

The building had windows that were still intact and ran high up along both the back and sides of those walls. The rain beat at them mercilessly, and the interior was bathed in murky shadows. From outside the wild, random firing stopped and Bolan heard men shout as they tried to organize themselves.

The Executioner knew it would only be moments before the men structured themselves into some semblance of order. As long as the MPCI rebels had ready access to narcotics, they would have no shortage of courage. His real concern was that they possessed communications capabilities competent enough to possibly alert du Toit and his men as to Bolan's location.

The windows set into the walls were too high for Bolan to use to escape. The empty floor of the building would offer him no cover when the guerrillas stormed the door. He was being driven like a wild animal into a pen.

Bolan turned and looked at the door. He had no choice. He ran to the interior door, tried the handle and found it locked. He stepped back and curled his leg up tight, snapped his leg out and kicked the door hard, striking it parallel to the handle with the heel of his combat boot.

The door popped open and swung wide, revealing a dark pit and an old ramshackle set of stairs leading down into darkness. A dank stench rolled up and assaulted Bolan's nose.

He stepped onto the first rickety stair, which groaned in protest under his weight. He took another step. The staircase seemed to be holding. Bolan had no overwhelming desire to be caught in a dark hole in the earth, but his options were running out.

He walked down several stairs, then turned and sank to his knees. He lowered himself down to his belly and stretched out, resting the muzzle of the AKM across the top stair. He commanded the only entrance to the building now.

Bolan felt adrenaline twist his guts. He hadn't been in a spot this tight in a while. He needed to attend to his wounds, needed people to stop shooting at him and needed to get the information on Saragossa's phone out to the right people. Most of all he needed to *not* be trapped like an animal in a hole.

He felt the stairs settle under his weight and heard them groan in protest. There'd been no way to determine how unsound the staircase was when he'd first entered the basement door, and now Bolan began to rethink his plan. Perhaps it would be wiser for him to relocate to a spot on the main floor at an angle to the front entrance.

Machine-gun fire riddled the frame around the front door even as the thought flashed through Bolan's mind. Green and white tracer fire arced into the room. He nestled in behind the buttstock of the AKM and drew down on the front door. He saw more streaks of green tracer fire fly through the doorway and the gray slashes as bullets cut through the dusty air.

Bolan tightened his finger on the trigger, taking in the slack. He narrowed his eyes and looked down the barrel of his weapon.

A baseball-sized sphere arced into the room. Bolan cursed as the hand grenade bounced off the floor, landed, and then rolled toward the center of the room. He put his head down and ducked underneath the lip of the stair.

Through his closed eyelids Bolan had an impression of a bright flash, then the explosion deafened him. He heard shrapnel strike the walls around the basement door and he opened his eyes and lifted his head. Dark smoke filled the room. The wooden staircase under his body shook with the concussive impact.

From the entrance Bolan heard more weapons fire and saw muzzle-flashes. After the initial bursts men screamed back and forth at one another and the first rebel entered the room, firing his weapon from the hip.

Bolan scythed the man down with a short burst, then shifted his weight and pointed his captured AKM back toward the door. A second MPCI gunman entered the building, and Bolan put a 3-round burst into his chest, knocking him straight back out the door. A gunman on the outside stuck his weapon into the room from around the door frame and began spraying wildly, trying to provide cover fire for a second entry team.

Screaming like a madman, another guerrilla burst into the room, firing his weapon from the hip as well. Bolan sighted in on him and pulled the AKM trigger. Two shots rang out and both struck the man in his torso, knocking him down but not killing him.

The AKM suddenly stopped firing despite Bolan's finger pressure on the trigger. Bolan broke his cheek seal with the butt of the weapon and looked at the weapon ejection port. He didn't see a miss feed. Across the room the wounded MPCI guerrilla rolled over onto his side and looked around.

Bolan automatically began to perform an immediate action drill on his weapon the way he had practiced a thousand times. He slapped up on the bottom of the AKM magazine to ensure it was seated properly, then pulled the weapon charging handle to the back all the way, locking the bolt to the rear. No jammed cartridge ejected.

The wounded gunman shouted something to others outside the door and lifted his own weapon, bringing it to bear on the doorway where Bolan had set up his hasty defensive position.

Bolan saw his chamber was clear and slid the charging handle forward and released the firing bolt from its locked position. He pointed his AKM up at the wounded guerrilla and pulled the trigger on the AKM just as the other man began firing as well.

The weapon failed to fire, and Bolan flinched as 7.62 mm rounds began hammering at his position. There was no time for him to perform a remedial action drill to try bringing the Kalashnikov back online. He twisted onto his side and pulled his Desert Eagle out of its holster.

Bolan had the .44 Magnum pistol ready to go, but the fire coming into the doorway was too intense for him to lift his head, much less bring the big hand cannon to bear. He shifted to avoid a flurry of splinters kicked up by enemy rounds, and he felt the staircase suddenly lurch under him.

The staircase groaned like an old man in pain, and Bolan felt it give way beneath him. As automatic weapons fire sprayed in an unending fusillade through the open basement door, Bolan fell into the darkness.

19

"I understand," du Toit said.

The mercenary broke the connection on the sat phone, rose from the bed and pulled on his pants. He looked over his shoulder at the girl as he buckled his belt.

"Get up," he said.

Listless, the girl rolled onto her back.

There was a knock on the door, and du Toit grunted for the person to enter. Johnston walked into the room, his weapon casually slung over one shoulder. He looked over at the half-naked girl who made no move to cover herself. There were purple bite marks on her shoulder.

Du Toit's group had taken over a house on the southern outskirts of Niangoloko, the closest town to the north of Yendere. They had left Yendere with Le Crème's men as Burkina army units had begun to enter that township. Ivory Coast forces had overrun the southern part of Yendere, sending in infantry units as soon as the rains had started again.

According to what Le Crème had been told by the army commander, the Ivory Coast forces held the mosque, the hotel and the combined UNICEF and Burkina customs offices. Lackluster fighting had broken out between the two national forces as each sought to press an advantage while international representatives brokered a cease-fire.

Predictably, the MPCI bands had begun slipping into the countryside to the west and east of the township. Du Toit had contacted his office in Pretoria, South Africa, which had instructed him to wait while the information about the situation was relayed to the principals.

Those principals had offered to pay the full amount of the contract again if the mysterious white commando who had apparently met with Saragossa before her death could be apprehended. A smaller sum was offered for his death.

"What is it, Johnston?" du Toit asked.

"Le Crème is outside."

"What does that fat bastard want?"

"He says the bleeding MPCI contacted one of his custom men still in Yendere. They say they have a white man cornered in a warehouse on the east side of the town, away from the main fighting."

Du Toit felt elation well up. He began buttoning his shirt, and stuffed his feet into his boots. A smile pulled at the corners of his mouth.

"Get the men ready," he ordered. "We're going back into Yendere. We may just make our bonuses after all."

Johnston grinned and then snuck a peek at the girl's bare, bruised breasts before turning to leave.

"I told you to get dressed!" Du Toit ordered the girl. "We'll see how your great *Gunab* does now," he said, sneering.

BOLAN FELL THROUGH THE HOLE in the rotted stairs and plummeted into the black below. As he fell he curled into a ball, drawing the Desert Eagle in close to prevent losing it. He struck something hard and bounced, spinning so that his head was above his feet. He struck the floor hard with his buttocks and rolled backward. His teeth snapped together and he felt the hot, metallic-tang of his own blood as he bit the inside of his cheek.

He was thrown onto his back, and his head hit a dirt floor. Bolan opened his eyes as dust and debris rained down on his upturned face. The open door ten or twelve feet above him stood out like a square of pale light in the murk.

A figure appeared suddenly, silhouetted in the opening. The shape raised a rifle and began to spray rounds into the basement. Still dizzy from the fall and impact, Bolan raised the Desert Eagle. He pointed the muzzle upward and aimed center mass on his target.

The hand cannon went off with a boom loud enough to deafen Bolan in the confined space. The muzzle-flash formed spots in Bolan's eyes. The figure, now simply a blurry smear against the backdrop of light, staggered backward. The rifle fell out of his hands and bounced off the ruined staircase. Bolan twisted to the side and instinctively lifted his arm over his head to avoid the falling rifle.

The weapon struck him hard in the shoulder and fell away. Bolan winced, hissing at the impact of the ten-pound assault rifle. It clattered as it struck the ground. Bolan rolled onto his back again. He slid the Desert Eagle into its holster by feel and snatched up the dropped assault rifle, some model of Kalashnikov.

A figure appeared in the door and Bolan just had time to bring the Kalashnikov to bear. Tracer fire ripped out of Bolan's weapon and shot through the dark pit he was trapped in. The rounds pierced the second gunman and knocked him back out of sight.

Bolan scrambled to his feet and moved toward the wall directly under the open door. His heart hammered in his chest as his eyes began to adjust, giving him a better impression of the basement he had tumbled into.

He looked up and saw that ruined stairs ran against one wall of the room. Remnants of the staircase hung from the door frame and dangled above him. On the other side of the hole he'd created when he'd fallen through it, the staircase was intact and ran down to the dirt floor of the basement.

Before he could take in any further details of the room he saw a familiar metal sphere fly through the door and drop toward him. Bolan exploded into action. He leaped forward as the grenade struck the ground at his feet and scooped it up.

Bolan spun out away from the wall and cocked his arm. He lobbed the cooking grenade back up toward the door, then threw himself back against the wall. The grenade sailed through the open door and exploded.

The explosion detonated loudly over Bolan's head, and he was grimly rewarded by the sound of screams. Their superior numbers had emboldened the guerrillas up to this point, but Bolan felt confident that they did not have the discipline or morale needed to commit to the kind of casualities it would take to pull him out of his hole. If they tried, then he would make them pay. It was that simple.

With the blast of the grenade still ringing in his ears, Bolan pushed himself off the wall. He scanned the area around him, trying to gain some sense as to the size of the basement. He could see immediately that he was dealing with a cavernous structure easily as large as the open bay directly above him.

The wide, open storage area was filled with items—shapes covered in canvas, rusting machinery, oil drums and construction materials on plywood pallets. Bolan fired a burst of harassing fire into the open door above him and quickly scrambled in among the mess.

Finding a position that offered him some cover, Bolan squatted and pulled out Saragossa's phone. He flipped it open and read the face. A white screen was broken by the words: NO SERVICE.

Bolan cursed and shut the phone. He hadn't really expected any better. With his sat phone he believed he could make contact with Grimaldi or Stony Man Farm if he needed, but it would do him little good in his current situation.

He put the phone away. His first order was to get to a location where he could send Saragossa's picture of her intelligence findings to another user and ensure the information got out. Then he'd find a way to get himself out.

The Executioner turned, lined up the rifle sights on the door and closed his left eye to spare his night vision before firing a burst. The harassing fire sprayed the open doorway and shot out into the warehouse floor beyond.

After the burst Bolan turned and forced his way farther into the basement. He moved toward the cellar wall and saw a series of metal pipes set in brackets running along the length of the basement and back into the darkness. He didn't allow himself to hope, but he felt a grim smile tug at the corners of his mouth. He thought it possible that he had just caught a break.

He reached up and touched the largest of the metal pipes, pulled his hand back and inspected his fingers. They were black with soot. This time he allowed the smile to linger. When it had been in use, the building had utilized a natural resource for energy that was in no short supply on the African continent. Coal. A coal furnace for an industrial site meant an industrial-sized supply depot as the coal would have arrived by the truckload. The coal chute for a furnace that size would be more than large enough for a man to crawl through.

Bolan began fighting his way toward the rear of the basement. It was hard going, made more arduous by the occasional guerrilla brave enough to broach the basement door. In the dark Bolan found the memory of Saragossa's puffy and infected arm had a worse effect on him than the ineffectual bullets of the poorly trained group of MPCI thugs. He wondered about the prospect of stumbling across a scorpion or a poisonous spider in the cramped, dank quarters.

He didn't see any insects, but his movement upset more than one nest of African bush rats and they squeaked at him angrily or hissed, their beady eyes reflecting red in the meager light. Bolan had no fear of rats, but he understood the ecosystem enough to be concerned by their presence. Bugs brought rats. Rats brought snakes. Perhaps poisonous.

Finally Bolan reached the other side of the basement and quickly began to search along the back wall. As he had suspected the furnace was huge, as big as an SUV, made of cast iron and covered in thick, black soot. Bolan wormed his way through the debris around it and found the coal chute. It ran up into the wall at a forty-five-degree angle from a railroad coal truck. Coal so old it had turned gray spilled over the edges of the bin and across the cellar floor. Cobwebs clung in thick curtains at the corners of the chute.

Bolan stepped forward and waved the hot muzzle of his rifle through the mess. Spiderwebs clung to his barrel, wrapping around it like cotton candy. Bolan scraped the webs off on the edge of the coal bin. Spiders the size of his thumbnail scurried out of the mess and across the lumps of old coal.

He bent down and looked up the coal chute, seeing a sliver of gloomy gray daylight at the top of the short tunnel where the chute hatch hung imperfectly on its ancient hinges. The tunnel was clogged with dense spiderwebs. It was an unappealing escape route.

He was far from a squeamish man, but Saragossa had died hard and those stings on her hand had contained poison that could easily kill a grown man. In Africa the insects were as deadly as land mines. It was no minor phobia that made Bolan question the chute.

Behind him he heard the crack of metal striking concrete and instinctively he hunched against the blast. The grenade explosion shook dust loose from the ceiling and it rained down on Bolan's head, enforcing a feeling of claustrophobic tension. Shrapnel scattered through the room, gouging chips out of the wall and cutting into the materials crammed into the basement.

An assault rifle opened up in the doorway and sprayed down into the darkness. Bolan squatted behind the furnace to avoid a stray bullet or ricochet. The MPCI fighters were showing slightly more tenacity than he had given them credit for.

Unless something is encouraging them to stay, Bolan thought. *Something like money funneled to their officers by a Burkina gendarme with connections outside the country.*

Du Toit's men would have the skills and tools necessary to simply drop the building down on Bolan's head, and they owed him for the mercenaries he had killed. That was the worst-case scenario.

In the best-case scenario the South Africans knew he had the information Saragossa had been sent to get and so would be willing to risk coming down after him. Bolan would have a greater chance then than if they simply blew the building down on him, but at least that way Saragossa's secret would die with him. Until Venezuela sent someone else to follow up.

Bolan had no choice. He had to get out.

He stepped around the corner of the furnace and lifted the rifle up above his head, angling the barrel of the weapon so that its trajectory would fire above the massive piles of industrial relics filling the huge basement.

He triggered an exploratory burst. His bullets arced out over the storage and sailed into the far wall and staircase remnants. Satisfied, Bolan fired a second, longer burst designed to encourage caution on the part of the MPCI fighters.

Bolan lowered his weapon and stepped back around the edge of the furnace. He eyed the choking mess of spiderwebs inside the old coal chute. If the wrong kind of spider inhabited the webs, then he was no better off than if he faced bullets. Dead was dead and worse, if the poison was strong but slow, Bolan would be too weak to fight off his captors as he lay dying. But there really was no choice.

Bolan set the rifle up against the coal bin and reached down into one of the cargo pockets of his pants and pulled a sealed pouch from it. Bolan tore the Velcro open and pulled out his lighter. He struck the lighter, and it caught on the first try.

Bolan leaned forward and touched the flame to the dangling cobwebs. The silky strands ignited immediately and went up with a surprisingly intense whoosh. He stepped back from the sudden flare and put away his lighter.

An explosion of insects poured out the mouth of the coal chute. They spilled over the lip, some displaying partially melted legs or singed bodies. Beetles, roaches, centipedes as long as Bolan's hand, and spiders of every size from that of a quarter to one as big as his fist scurried away from the sudden heat and light.

Bolan snatched up the AKM and stepped back to keep the avalanche of bugs from spilling across his boots. Brown smoke roiled out of the chute as ancient coal dust caught fire, intensifying the flames. A burst of machine-gun fire erupted from the basement door, but Bolan ignored it, watching the hundreds of insects spilling out of his homemade inferno.

The fire raced through the mesh of webs, spurred by the

coal dust residue trapped in the chute. Bolan looked in and could see the grisly lumps of all the things that had not crawled to safety.

The last flame snuffed out up the chute at the end by the hatch to the outside. Bolan lifted his leg and stepped into the coal bin. The coal shifted under his weight, dislodging creatures in a second desperate exodus. Bolan ignored it.

He waded across the coal bin to the still smoking mouth of the chute, changing his fire-selector switch to safe. He hung the rifle around his neck by the sling, muzzle down so the barrel would drag between his legs as he crawled up the gutter.

Bolan eyed the run. It was large enough to accommodate him but narrow enough that he would be forced to scramble up it using his elbows and knees to dig into the corners. He drew the Beretta 93-R from his shoulder holster and stuck his upper body into the opening.

The sides of the coal chute were still warm, but Bolan shoved himself inside and began to inch his way up the enclosure. His pant leg caught on a jagged section of metal in the opening and he jerked his leg to clear it. He heard the ripping sound as his pants tore, but his leg came free.

Bolan continued climbing. With every movement of his elbow or knee he cracked the seared shell of some insect and guts smeared into the material of his clothes. He took shallow breaths through his mouth.

It was close and fetid, but Bolan finally reached the end of the chute and twisted his body, pinning his hips and knees against the sides of the chute to acquire leverage.

He took his free hand and pushed against the chute door, which was the size of a large coffee table. It opened about a quarter of an inch, and Bolan realized that smoke had to have billowed out of the opening during the brief fire. It could have easily attracted the attention of people outside the building.

Bolan listened for a moment, acutely aware of how vulnerable his position had become. All he could hear was the sound of the rainfall with its monotonous hammering. He had gone too far now to turn back. Cocking his hand, Bolan struck the chute door with all his strength.

There was a screech of metal on metal and the chute door sagged abruptly, then opened about a foot. Bolan drew back his hand and thrust it forward again. A bottom hinge popped off like a gun shot and Bolan scrambled out.

He slid through the gap headfirst and fell a few feet into the weeds and mud against the side of the big building. He rolled immediately and lifted the Beretta, tracking for targets. He saw nothing and turned in a tight circle, covering all points.

The rain hammered into him, and once again Bolan felt grateful for its incessant company. He looked at his surroundings and saw he was standing next to a concrete loading dock in the middle of knee-high weeds. A narrow alley ran between the warehouse he had just escaped and an almost identical building set across from it. Bolan turned toward the front of the building where the alley met the street on which the MPCI fighters had set up their roadblock.

Not wanting to be spotted by reinforcements coming to the aid of the gunmen who'd trapped him in the warehouse, Bolan spun on his heel and sprinted up the alley in the opposite direction. He scooped up the dangling AKM in one hand and clicked it off safe as he holstered the Beretta 93-R.

He crossed the muddy alley and turned the corner of the second warehouse. He saw a large Quonset hut with a sliding door that had obviously served as a vehicle garage at one time.

A mortar shell had torn a hole in its side and blown out the windows. He heard automatic weapons firing in an almost continuous barrage from several blocks over.

Bolan crawled under a loose section of chain-link fence and scrambled into the building through the blast hole. He scanned the interior of the building, tracking with the assault rifle. Nothing moved. A large tow truck showing obvious signs of damage from the mortar round filled the hut. Other than that, Bolan was alone.

He leaned back against the wall and closed his eyes, exhausted and thirsty. Dehydration was a critical factor and had sapped the strength of many strong, fit men. Finding water would have to be his top priority.

Almost.

Bolan reached down to a cargo pocket and opened it. Outside of the warehouse he might be able to get a signal from Saragossa's cell phone. He reached inside but felt nothing. Frowning, Bolan pushed his hand deeper and his fingers found the ragged hole at the bottom of his pocket.

The entire bottom of the cargo pocket on his leg had been ripped open and the contents had spilled out. Saragossa's phone was gone. He suddenly remembered catching his leg on the lip of the coal chute as he had begun his climb. The phone had to have been lost then.

Bolan cursed. He was going to have to go back into the coal chute and down into the basement. For a minute he almost considered leaving it. Surely no other operation in the past had ever been plagued by such bizarre and unlikely mishaps. Maybe someone was trying to tell him something. You can't win 'em all, Bolan thought.

His throat suddenly constricted as if he were physically choking at the mere thought of such defeat. Bolan felt a flush of anger burn through his fatigued body. No, you couldn't win them all, he realized. But there was one hell of a difference between going down fighting and simply quitting.

The Executioner might die, but he would never quit.

20

"That the building?" du Toit asked.

The South African looked at the warehouse through the sweeping rhythm of the windshield wipers as the motorcade pulled onto the Yendere street.

"That's what they say," Le Crème answered.

His gendarmes spilled out of the vehicles behind them and began to make contact with the group of MPCI fighters who had taken up positions in and around the building.

"They manage to get him yet?"

"Apparently he's trapped in the basement and is resisting their efforts," the colonel replied.

Du Toit snorted and got out of the vehicle. Johnston ran up to him and du Toit wasted no time in directing the other mercenary to take some men and reconnoiter the warehouse from all sides as it was readily apparent that the MPCI guerrillas had succumbed to tunnel vision in their efforts and concentrated on the basement door to the exclusion of other possibilities.

He watched as a rebel fighter conferred with Le Crème who listened closely, unmindful of the rain, then nodded vigorously when the man finished speaking.

"What did he say?" du Toit demanded.

"He says that they have stopped receiving answering fire

to their grenades a little while ago. They believe him to be badly wounded or dead."

Du Toit frowned. He watched Johnston direct some of the South African mercenaries down the street in front of the building before taking another man and entering the alley directly in front of where the motorcade was parked.

"Let's go inside," du Toit said.

"Fine," Le Crème answered. "The main floor is perfectly safe in any event, as they have the entrance covered."

"You fix things with the army?"

"Troops have been instructed not to enter this part of the city. A cease-fire has been brokered by the UN, and the army is waiting to retake the government buildings in the town center."

Du Toit nodded absently. Things moved quickly when neither side was particularly interested in continuing the fight. He turned and looked at the girl who sat listlessly in the back of the car. He slapped the top of the car with the flat of his hand, and she slowly turned her head to regard him. Her left eye was swollen shut.

"You stay in this car," du Toit ordered. "You understand?"

The girl nodded.

"Say it," he snapped. "Say I understand."

"I understand," she mumbled.

"Louder!"

"I understand."

"You're goddamn right you do." Du Toit slammed the car door and began to stalk toward the front of the building, his AK-104 gripped loosely in one hand.

"Look out, Mr. Gunab," he muttered. "Here I come."

BOLAN CROUCHED IN THE RAIN and watched the South African team sweep around the warehouse. Four men entered the alley where the coal chute was located, moving in a loose overwatch formation. Two of the men took up positions in the alleyway while the second team swept around the back of the building.

Bolan faded back around behind the Quonset hut where he had holed up. He circled it, then left the area through an open gate in the chain-link fence. He slipped over to the edge of the second warehouse and hugged the wall as he moved up to the mouth of the alley, completely out of sight of the team pulling security there.

The Executioner caught a flash of movement ahead of him through the driving rain, and he stopped moving and sank to one knee against the building. He narrowed his eyes and was able to make out the last man of the first team as he rounded the corner on the far side of the first warehouse.

Bolan rose and continued to make his way toward the alley mouth. The Quonset hut where he had stopped momentarily now lay on his right side, surrounded by the dilapidated chain-link fence he had crawled under. He reached the corner of the second warehouse and stopped, back up against the wall.

Holding the AKM muzzle up, Bolan quickly looked around the corner, then snatched his head back. He internalized what he had seen, placing each of the mercenaries performing security on that side of the old warehouse into a precise mental picture. Beyond the mercs Bolan had caught a glimpse of a vehicle he recognized as the one Le Crème and du Toit had driven to Kibidwe Hotel earlier. As far as Bolan had been able to see across the distance and through the rain, no one had been in the Land Rover or on the main street.

What he proposed to do was so obviously risky it was almost beyond the need of acknowledgment. But Bolan acknowledged it, accepted it and then executed it.

He let the AKM hang across his body, around his neck and over his left shoulder. The muzzle pointed straight down by his leg with the pistol grip riding snug to his right hip. He pulled the Beretta 93-R out of his shoulder holster the way he had a thousand times before and took the deadly Italian pistol in both hands.

Bolan came around the corner and extended the silenced weapon before him. Two white mercenaries crouched on either side of the obviously broken coal chute hatch, facing each other. Sensing movement, the merc facing in Bolan's direction looked up.

The Executioner saw the mercenary's eyes narrow as he scrambled to lift his weapon, an HK-94 with its stock folded down. The man opened his mouth to shout a warning as he lifted the assault carbine. Bolan shot him between the eyes at fifteen yards.

The man's head jolted back as if he'd been punched, and blood spilled down over the bridge of his nose and ran down his cheek and into his beard as he slumped downward. The sound of the slide racking another round into the chamber on the Beretta was lost in the driving rain.

The mercenary with his back to Bolan saw his partner go down and tried to turn. He was too slow by a country mile. Bolan's shot struck the man in the temporal lobe of his skull, and the 9 mm Parabellum round cracked his head like an egg. The man slumped to the side, dropping his weapon and falling to the ground.

Still charging forward, Bolan holstered the Beretta. He reached the coal chute and grabbed the broken hatch with both hands. Kicking one foot against the warehouse wall, Bolan pulled with all his strength, bending the door back on its single good hinge.

Grabbing the corpses, Bolan heaved the first one up and shoved him down the chute. Without waiting to see what happened Bolan whirled and snatched up the second dead man. He turned and muscled the body up before shoving it head-first down the coal run as well.

Satisfied, Bolan removed the AKM and took it up in one hand. He stepped toward the coal chute and was prepared to slide down when he heard a car door slam. Bolan spun back toward the front mouth of the alley and lifted the Kalashnikov, his finger finding the smooth curve of the trigger.

The girl stood in the mouth of the alley. She stood unmoving in the rain as it pelted into her, soaking her to the bone in seconds. Her hands hung loosely at her sides, and Bolan could see she wasn't armed. Their eyes met across the distance, and she made no move to call out a warning shout to anyone nearby.

Bolan felt a chill enter his heart. The girl began walking toward him, and he lowered the AKM. She would be an easy shot with the Beretta, but he made no move to draw the pistol. As she drew closer, Bolan could make out the bruises on her face and knew instinctively who had put them there.

He shook his head at her and she stopped walking. Not entirely sure of what he was doing or why he was doing it, Bolan held up his hand, palm toward her. "Stop," he whispered, and she stood there for a heartbeat before nodding once, slowly.

Bolan turned back to the coal chute. He crouched and balanced on one hand before sticking both feet up and sliding back down the chute run and into the warehouse basement.

The big man slid easily. The chute had been lubricated by the spilling blood of the men he'd shot. He landed in the coal bin on top of the two bodies and brought up his AKM. He heard gunfire immediately and saw muzzle-flashes coming from the doorway across the clutter-filled basement.

Shapes silhouetted themselves in the door and then leaped down into the room. Bolan cursed. The mercenaries hadn't wasted any time in assaulting the basement. He flung the AKM assault rifle away from him and snatched up a dead merc's AK-104.

The size of a submachine gun, the shortened 104 model was still chambered for the 7.62 mm round. That meant AKM and AK-47 magazines fit the weapon well, and since Bolan was scavenging his ammunition, that was a huge bonus as 7.62 mm rounds were abundant in the slaughterhouse Yendere had become.

Bolan sat up and quickly inspected the weapon to ensure it was ready for firing. He ignored the approaching killers on the far side of the crowded room. He thrust his hands out into the coal pile, mindful of the stream of insects that had scurried out of the coal chute earlier.

He felt around in the uncertain light, groping for the lost cell phone. Behind him he heard the mercs calling out to each other in Afrikaans. Bolan looped the AK-104 around his neck, then picked up his discarded AKM.

Turning slightly, Bolan lifted the AKM and fired a long burst that burnt off the magazine in the assault rifle. He needed to make the mercenary soldiers cautious enough to slow their advance, even if in his current position he would be unlikely to strike any targets.

Bolan heard men cursing and calling back and forth to one another in the wake of his burst. He tossed the spent AKM aside and began to search through the now blood drenched lumps of coal. Something with what felt like a hundred legs scurried across his hand.

From behind him someone fired a short burst with a submachine gun, but the bullets were soaked up by the massive structure of the coal furnace. Then Bolan heard something metal strike the ground behind him amid the scattered materials in the basement.

Bolan dived forward and rolled, pulling one of the corpses over himself. The explosion came a heartbeat later as the grenade detonated. From the sound of the explosion and the rain of steel that followed, Bolan ascertained that the little bomb had been a fragmentation grenade. A safer choice given the potentially unstable structure above them than a high explosive variation would have been.

Shrapnel struck all around him, and he felt the vibration through the corpse as it soaked up a few of the jagged missiles. Bolan picked up the AK-104 and fired. He angled the muzzle to the ceiling and out toward the middle of the room, hoping to bounce his rounds into the South Africans.

A burst fired in response to his, but again the bullets were mostly deflected by the furnace. Bolan needed time he did not have. His mind raced as he sought to come up with some sort of a plan.

"Don't shoot!" he yelled.

He continued to feel around with his hands among the sliding pile of coal. He could sense the hesitation his communication had caused. "Don't shoot!" he repeated. "I want to negotiate."

There was a murmur of voices in response to his declaration. Bolan's fingers touched something smooth and metal. Disappointment washed over him when he realized what he had found and lifted his lighter, slipping it back into a pocket.

From the door to the basement he heard du Toit's voice. It grated on his nerves, and he had to stop himself from turning and trying to put a bullet through the mercenary leader.

"Negotiate what?" du Toit demanded.

"I'm hit," Bolan lied.

"That's not my problem. My problem is lying bloody well dead in a hotel room not too far from here."

"I have her laptop," Bolan lied again. He shoved the two bodies out of his way and began to search the area that had been covered by them. "It has the information she was supposed to give to her principals."

"*That* I might be interested in," du Toit allowed. "But I can get that off your corpse."

"You fire on me again," Bolan warned, "you throw another grenade, and I'll blow this thing apart. Understand? You'll get nothing."

"I'll get the money they're paying me to kill you for screwing up their operation."

"They'll give you more for what I have," Bolan stated.

"And just who the hell *are* you?" du Toit demanded.

Bolan didn't bother to answer. He found Saragossa's phone in the coal pile and slid it into the breast pocket of his shirt and worked the button closed. He shifted his weapon so that it hung behind him over his shoulder. He crawled over the dead men to the mouth of the chute. He called out over his shoulder and back into the depths of the basement.

"Do we have a deal or not?" Bolan shouted. "This is just a paycheck to me, but I'll damn well destroy the laptop if you keep jerking me around."

After a moment of silence du Toit said, "Let's deal."

"I'm coming out," Bolan yelled. "Give me a second, I'm hurt and it'll take a minute. I'll tell you whatever you want to know."

"One wrong move and we'll blow you away," du Toit warned.

Bolan didn't bother to continue the charade. Having negotiated his reprieve through misdirection, he ducked his head under the top lip of the coal chute and began to climb his way out of the basement.

21

The Executioner scrambled up the crawlspace, panting from the exertion in the humidity and heat. He reached the top and quickly peered around the corner of the coal chute. The alley was empty, and the girl was nowhere to be seen.

Good, Bolan thought, it makes things simpler.

He slid out of the chute and back onto the muddy ground of the alley. He heard a car engine race and he looked up, bringing the AK-104 to the ready.

Le Crème's Land Rover rushed into the alley. Bolan shifted the AK-104 and took aim. He saw the girl hunched behind the wheel, her face as impassive as ever. Her cool aloofness was an enigma to Bolan, and he found himself admiring her stark, simple courage.

Bolan flattened himself against the wall of the warehouse as the girl braked and the speeding Land Rover slid to a stop in front of him. She twisted in her seat and reached back to open the rear door to the stolen vehicle.

"Get in!" she ordered in French.

Bolan scrambled for the door. As he did so, two gendarmes sprinted around the corner at the front of the alley. They yelled something and began firing from the hip. Bullets struck the Land Rover and shattered the back windshield. Rounds struck showers of sparks like flint on steel as they caromed off the warehouse walls and the roof of the Land Rover.

Bolan dropped to one knee and lifted his AK-104. While the gendarmes wildly sprayed their weapons, barely in control of them, Bolan coolly aimed his Kalashnikov. The Executioner's initial burst knocked the weapon out of the hands of the gendarme on the left and then punched into his stomach, folding him over and dumping him to the ground.

Finger still holding down on his trigger, Bolan smoothly swept his weapon to the right and stitched a line of slugs across the second gendarme's chest. Scarlet blossoms erupted on the khaki uniform blouse and the man staggered backward under their impact, firing his weapon into the ground.

"Come on!" the girl screamed.

Bolan dived into the back of the Land Rover, landing on broken glass from the shattered rear windshield. The girl gunned the vehicle and its tires spun in the mud. The rear end fishtailed as she found purchase and the Land Rover shot forward. The open door banged and bounced off the warehouse wall before slamming shut as the girl sped away.

"Turn right, turn right!" Bolan ordered in French.

The girl jerked the wheel hard and shot down the narrow alley dividing the second warehouse from the chain-link fence surrounding the Quonset hut where Bolan had briefly gone to ground.

"Do you know a way out of here?" Bolan asked. "One that doesn't involve roadblocks or government troops?"

The girl nodded. "I think so."

The girl fought to keep the Land Rover under control. Her driving was out of control. They shot out of the alley and onto a road. She cornered too sharply, and Bolan felt the driver-side tires lift off the road. He opened his mouth to order her to pull over so he could take the wheel.

"My God!" she shouted. "They are coming!"

Bolan turned in the seat and saw Burkina gendarme vehicles burst out into the street about a hundred yards behind them. The vehicles were closed cab, so no weapons had been mounted on them, but men hung out of the car windows despite the driving rain, and the vehicles fairly bristled with their weapons.

"Drive!" Bolan shouted, not believing his own ears.

He laid the muzzle of his short-barreled Kalashnikov across the seat rest of the Land Rover and tried to draw a bead despite the relentless bouncing the vehicle was being subjected to.

He fired an exploratory burst but saw the rounds go wide and to the right. The officer riding shotgun in the lead gendarme vehicle returned fire, but his rounds flew as wild as Bolan's had.

The Executioner drew one knee up under him and attempted to steady himself by extending his other leg so that his foot was jammed under the back of the front passenger seat. He sighted down the muzzle of the AK-104, now cursing the shortened barrel, which reduced his accuracy over distance.

Bolan triggered a blast and saw mud kick up in front of the gendarme vehicle. He fired a longer blast and let the muzzle climb with the recoil of his rounds. The girl drove through a series of potholes and jostled Bolan across the back seat as he fired.

He saw a single round from his burst spiderweb the lead chase vehicle's windshield up near the roof. The men in the rear seats hung out their windows and returned fire. Their rounds passed harmlessly overhead.

The girl cut the stolen Land Rover sharply again and Bolan was catapulted off the passenger door and back into the middle of the seat. He fought to right himself and bring the Kalashnikov to bear. The vehicles behind them were less than seventy-five yards away and closing fast.

Bolan tried to take aim, but the vehicle moved too erratically for him to level a clean shot. Splinters of broken glass cracked under the pressure of his knee as he dug it into the seat, trying to steady himself. The girl hit another pothole, and the top of Bolan's head slammed into the cab roof.

"Stop!" he yelled. "Just stop!"

The girl did not argue. She did not even hesitate. She slammed on the vehicle's brake pedal with both her feet. The Toyota went into an immediate skid. Bolan was thrown hard up against the back of the driver seat, then fell back and landed again on the rear seat.

He lifted the AK-104 and triggered a burst from the now stationary platform. The rounds flew true, right straight into the front grille of the gendarme vehicle bearing down on them. Even through the falling rain Bolan could see the sudden plume of white steam as his rounds tore into the Land Rover's radiator.

"Go!" Bolan yelled.

Again the girl did not question, but simply responded. She rammed her foot on the gas and the Land Rover leaped forward. Bolan threw out an arm and grasped the headrest of the front passenger seat to keep from being thrown around like a rag doll in the back.

Behind him the lead chase vehicle veered suddenly to the right and rolled to a stop. The second vehicle was following too closely for the conditions and the driver's responses were not quick enough to avoid a collision. The vehicle tried pulling out to the left of the Land Rover Bolan had disabled, but wasn't fast enough. The rear vehicle tore off the lead Land

Rover's bumper and spun the vehicle like a top. One of the gendarmes who had been firing out of the back window was thrown clear.

The Burkina gendarme landed hard in the mud. The man lay in the road, stunned for a single breath before the third Land Rover in the caravan shot over his body and crushed his head like a melon.

The two vehicles following Bolan now didn't slow, but gunned it hard to try to catch up with their prey. Bolan turned his head to the side. He saw the lines of shanties and single-story silos on the outskirts of Yendere's east side fall away behind them.

The girl cleared the edge of the little West African border town and gunned the vehicle out into the grassland. Behind them gunmen in their vehicles rocked their weapons wide open on full-auto.

Bolan's vehicle struck an exposed stone in the road and the frame shuddered. The rear of the Land Rover shifted under the impact, and Bolan heard the unmistakable sound of the rear passenger-side tire blowing out.

The back of the already shaky vehicle lurched as the deflated tire struck the mud and then bounced. Bolan felt the vehicle's rear suspension rebound, and he knew they were going over. The Land Rover suddenly slid sideways, lifted into the air, then began to roll.

Bolan dropped his Kalashnikov and tried to grab the back of the front passenger seat. He missed and was thrown back. The vehicle shuddered as the roof struck the ground and crumpled inward.

The windshield shattered, but some distant part of Bolan's mind recognized that he couldn't hear the girl screaming. The vehicle came to rest on its driver's side.

Finding the AK-104, the big American snatched it up and twisted around from where he was crammed against the shattered rear passenger-side window. He struggled to get his feet under him. Nothing was happening in the front where the windshield had come apart.

"Are you okay?" Bolan asked.

He got no answer and he repeated the question in French. He looked down and saw blood spilling into the back along the ground. It pooled in around the soles of his boots where they stood on the shattered glass of the door window.

Bolan stuck his head through the space in between the seats. He looked down. The girl appeared pitiful in death, her small body lay limp, crumpled into a loose fetal position. Her neck was cocked at a disturbing angle and Bolan's guts churned. Her eyes were blank and fixed and stared straight out the shattered windshield.

Blood streamed out of her mouth and pooled beneath her head. Her body sighed reflexively, settling into death and the air rushed out of her lungs in a gasp. Her head sagged a little, and Bolan was suddenly able to see where the jagged end of her spine had thrust through the skin at the back of her neck.

The Executioner scrambled over the seats and out through the broken windshield. He crawled out of the wrecked Land Rover and stood. The vehicle's wheels were still spinning, but Bolan didn't notice.

He stalked toward the front of the gendarme Land Rover. He didn't notice the falling rain. Adrenaline infused his system but he felt calm, protected, even isolated from the danger around him in his self-created cocoon of impending justice.

The two trailing gendarme chase vehicles skidded to a stop, forming an off-center V. Bolan walked directly toward them, lifting the AK-104. Gunmen threw open doors and spilled out of the vehicles. The Executioner began to fire.

Bullets cut through the rain and sliced through the humid air around him. Bolan swept the muzzle of the AK-104, pouring fire into the front of the Land Rover on his left. He had never heard the dead girl utter the word *"Gunab,"* would not have understood what she meant even if he had. But now, in this place, in this time, the spirit of *Gunab* had entered Bolan and he fought like a man possessed.

His 7.62 mm rounds streamed through the left vehicle's windshield and pinned the driver to the seat. Bolan continued walking toward the vehicle as he fired. He shifted the Kalashnikov submachine gun at his hip and drilled the gunman hiding behind the open front passenger door. Bolan cut loose through the open cab of the Land Rover as he shifted aim. The high-velocity slugs ripped through the seats and into the back of the vehicle at a sharp angle, passing out the open rear passenger door and striking the gunman crouched there in his groin and thighs.

The man went down screaming. He triggered a blast with his AKM that pounded six rounds into the unprotected back of his comrade, who was firing on Bolan from behind the front passenger door of the Land Rover. The man shuddered under their impact and spasmed into an awkward pirouette. Bolan put four more slugs into the spinning man.

Bolan shifted in midstride and began spraying fire at the second vehicle. Bullets whipped around him from less than twenty yards away. He could see the muzzle-flashes flaring like sun spots, but he was deaf to the sound of their firing.

He wielded his Kalashnikov in a sloppy figure eight, raining fire down on the gunmen closest to him. His rounds struck the men and punched through the light skin of the vehicle doors, driving them back into the Land Rover. Shell casings spun out in an arc, bouncing off his bicep and tumbling like loose change onto the dirt road.

He felt the jolt in his hands as the rifle fired its last round and the bolt locked back in the open position. Bolan threw his empty weapon to the ground. On the other side of the vehicle the driver's weapon jammed and the stricken man also threw his rifle to the ground. Unlike Bolan, he turned and ran.

The man firing from the rear corner of the SUV turned his head to watch his comrade flee. He turned back and tried to trap Bolan in his weapon sights. He saw the ghostly killer lift a handgun in a smooth draw from the holster strapped to his thigh.

The man felt a freezing terror as he saw the muzzle on the .44 Magnum hand cannon. The Desert Eagle roared in Bolan's hand and a blaze of flame flashed like a sword of fire. The bullet punched through the door frame of the Land Rover as if it were paper and struck the man in his gut, shoving him back.

The roar of the pistol was like a thunderclap. The man screamed in agony at the searing pain plunging through his abdomen. Bolan's pistol jumped in his hand again, but the wounded Burkina gunman never heard the shot.

The round struck him square in his screaming face with sledgehammer force and flipped him over backward. The man lay faceup in the grass with the falling rain filling up the bloody cavity where his face had been.

The .44-caliber gunshots had cracked on the edge of Bolan's fugue, and he could feel himself being drawn forward into the here-and-now. He felt the sting of falling rain, then the dull throb of a wound high on the outside of his thigh. From behind him he heard a wounded man moaning and the hiss of escaping steam from a perforated engine block.

Time rushed back into Bolan like a tornado and everything he had just accomplished slammed into his consciousness in a whirlwind of images. He saw the dead girl's face again, pitiful in repose.

He ran forward and threw his arm across the still warm hood of the Land Rover. He sighted down the barrel of the Desert Eagle and planted his sights dead between the shoulder blades of the fleeing man. Bolan pulled the trigger on his pistol and the .44 roared in his hands.

Out in the grass the Burkina driver was thrown forward and landed facedown on the grass. The man lay on the ground as red soaked his uniform shirt. His leg kicked once then the body tensed up and finally relaxed.

Bolan stood. He dropped the magazine out of the Desert Eagle and slid a new one into place. He racked the slide and jacked a new round into the chamber. The Executioner carefully holstered the big pistol. He looked down at a dead man lying at his feet and saw a canteen on the man's web gear.

Bolan squatted and pulled it from its pouch. He spun off the cap, sniffed the contents, then greedily drank some of the tepid fluid. He drank as he rose slowly back to his feet, finishing the water by the time he was erect again. Bolan threw the empty canteen by the side of the road. He was covered in his own sweat despite the rain.

He looked over at the vehicle perched on its side in the middle of the road. He thought about the teenage girl lying dead inside, her neck snapped like a matchstick. Bolan drew the Beretta from his shoulder holster and took aim at the vehicle's exposed undercarriage.

The thought of those animal hands on the fragile body of the girl filled Bolan with icy certainty and resolve. The gas tank seemed as big as a bathtub in Bolan's experienced bead. His first 9 mm round pierced the tank. Gas began to pour out in an amber stream. His second round penetrated the tank and the scrape of bullet on metal lit a spark that ignited the gas fumes inside the tank.

The car went up like a Roman candle. Bolan turned his face away from the sudden flash of searing heat as burning pieces of wreckage came raining down into the mud. Black smoke roiled up in a column as flames engulfed the vehicle.

Bolan watched the vehicle burn with graveyard eyes.

From the ditch on the other side of the first vehicle Bolan had shot up, a wounded man continued moaning in agony. Bolan lowered the Beretta 93-R to his side. With his other hand he searched for Saragossa's phone. He found it, pulled it clear and flipped it open. A bitterly ironic smile tugged at his death mask—there was a signal.

Using his thumb, Bolan scrolled through the options and opened the picture file. He clicked the down arrow until he got the picture Saragossa had taken of her one page, handwritten report. Bolan sent a copy of the picture to Grimaldi's phone where the man was based out of Mali. He sent another one to Barbara Price's phone on the off chance it would make it. Now, even if he didn't make it out of this hellhole, the matter of the Iraqi laboratory would be taken care of.

Satisfied, he scrolled through the Numbers Called display and deleted the numbers before closing the phone. He moved his thumb to turn off the power and save the battery. The screen flashed a brief text message and he gritted his teeth in frustration when he saw the messages had failed to deliver.

Some instinct made him look up then, and he saw a line of vehicles racing out of the city toward him. Then a bullet hit his leg with crushing impact. Bolan's legs were swept out from under him and the muddy road flew up to meet him, slamming him hard in the face.

Bolan grunted at the impact and the world spun around him like a carnival ride. He heard the sound of a gunshot and looked up. He saw the gendarme he had wounded stretched out on the ground about fifteen yards from him. The man held a pistol in his hand and was firing from underneath the vehicle. Mud splashed up into Bolan's face as pistol rounds burrowed into the earth inches from his head.

Bolan rolled over once and swept the Beretta around. The wounded gendarme under the car was screaming as he pulled the trigger on his pistol. The Executioner stroked the trigger on the Beretta, squeezing harder than was prudent for accuracy but too juiced on his adrenaline to check the response.

The Beretta jumped in his hand as he unloaded the rest of his clip at the already wounded gunman. Bullets flew under the Land Rover as the two men shot at each other. Bolan saw blood geyser as his rounds struck the gunner in the chest and shoulders. The man sagged to the earth, limp and silent.

Knowing he couldn't afford to hesitate Bolan forced himself to his feet. He looked up. The second convoy of vehicles racing out of the city was less than a hundred yards away. Bolan shoved the cell phone into a pocket and hobbled toward the only vehicle undamaged enough to still drive. His leg bled freely and wouldn't work properly.

He looked down at the wound but couldn't tell how bad it was because of all the blood. Bolan fell forward into the open passenger door and crawled across the glass-littered seat and slid behind the wheel. The keys dangled from the ignition and the engine was still running.

Bolan heard the sound of gunfire behind him. He threw the vehicle's automatic transmission into drive and used his left leg to stomp on the gas. The vehicle raced away and threw mud in a shower behind it. With all four doors still hanging open, Bolan sped around the flaming wreck of the first Land Rover and back onto the road.

He lifted the Beretta and hit the magazine release with his

thumb, ejecting the spent clip onto the floor of the bloody cab. He stuck the gun in his lap and took the wheel with his right hand as he used his left to reach across his chest and pull a fresh magazine from his shoulder harness.

His leg felt as if it were on fire, and Bolan knew he had to stop the bleeding soon or what he'd endured was all for nothing. He took the wheel in his left hand and grabbed the fresh magazine with his right. Like a crime-scene detective lancing a spent shell casing with a ballpoint pen, Bolan slid the magazine into the pistol butt. Grabbing the Beretta, he tapped the magazine into place on the dash and then hit the slide release, chambering a round.

The Land Rover jerked and bounced under his hand as he took the ruined road too fast for safety. He heard more gunfire and he looked into his rearview mirror. The Land Rovers were gaining on him, and he could clearly see the yellow flashes of weapons fire through the gray streaks of falling rain.

Bolan realized he wasn't going to make it.

22

As du Toit's Land Rover swerved to avoid the burning vehicle in the middle of the road, he turned his head to watch it. He'd seen the foreign operator commandeer the gendarme vehicle as Le Crème's force had closed in on the battle scene. There had been no sign of the girl. Something deep in his gut, a warrior's instinct perhaps, told him she was in the burning pyre.

"This is becoming a very real problem," Le Crème snarled. "How am I supposed to explain my dead men to my superiors?"

Du Toit turned his attention back to the furious gendarme colonel. The sleepy-eyed man held his burning cigar between two thick fingers and he jabbed it over the seat at du Toit as he shouted.

The South African was unimpressed by the display of bluster, but he really didn't blame the man. The whole Yendere situation had turned into a disaster, and there was little use trying to deny it.

"This man is a danger to the state security of Burkina Faso. He is obviously here at the behest of an outside influence bent on destabilizing the government. You have plainly, through the sound use of basic police work, uncovered a Western plot. You're a fucking hero, Le Crème," du Toit said calmly.

The colonel's face relaxed as the implications of what du Toit was saying hit home. He slowly put his cigar in his mouth and bit down on the butt.

Sensing an advantage, du Toit pushed ahead with that line of reasoning. "You bag this guy, you put a bullet into his face. You parade his corpse on television. When that happens you'll be the president's number-one man just like *that*." Du Toit held his hand up and snapped his fingers for emphasis.

Subdued, Le Crème turned around in his seat. He liked what he was hearing and du Toit could see that. That was good, because if the son of a bitch thought he was pulling his resources out now he was sadly mistaken.

It was that simple.

Du Toit seethed. He'd lost all but three of his men as they'd pursued the foreigner. The man had killed his whore, humiliated him and literally taken bread out of his family's mouth by screwing up the operation. Now his bribe-loving sponsor was getting gun shy?

That smelled like prison to du Toit, and it would be a cold day in Africa before he went back to some stinking third-world prison. He remembered the way the whore had looked at him. The way her face had seemed to challenge him, as if to say nothing he did could touch the real her, the one inside. His hands itched to beat her now, and he couldn't.

He couldn't because *Gunab* had taken her from him.

"We'll get him," he promised.

Le Crème nodded from the front seat. "We better, my friend, or all the money on the continent won't buy us out of our trouble," he said.

"We'll get him," du Toit repeated.

He looked out through the furiously working windshield

wipers at the battered Land Rover racing over the ruined road just ahead of them. Three of the doors still hung open and most of the vehicle's windows had been shattered by gunfire.

Le Crème's driver, a badly frightened sergeant over six feet tall and all of 170 pounds, was pushing the chase but the rains had so rutted the road that he could barely keep his vehicle out of the ditch at the current speed.

Du Toit forced himself to be patient. He longed to hang out his window and fire at the fleeing Land Rover, but he knew under these conditions such actions would be futile, a sign of weakness. He refused to give into such base emotion. He was a professional and he would conduct himself as such.

Du Toit's hands massaged the weapon he held across his lap, squeezing and releasing, squeezing and releasing. His hate was like a bitter pill that he kept chewing but could not swallow.

"What's up ahead?" he asked Le Crème. "Anything that'll slow the bastard down?"

"The east road crosses the main railroad tracks," Le Crème shouted back. "After that the road simply gets worse."

"We'll get him."

"You keep saying that and it might even happen," Le Crème snorted.

The Land Rover hit a rut in the road and both Le Crème and du Toit were thrown hard against their doors. The driver managed to straighten the vehicle but when he was through fighting the steering wheel they were no closer to their quarry than they had been. Du Toit fairly gnashed his teeth in frustration.

"We'll get him."

BOLAN REACHED OUT and snatched up the AKM. Once it was across his lap he bent down and pulled his knife from the sheath in his boot. He looked up and swerved to avoid a gigantic pothole. The primitive conditions of the road were killing him, tearing the vehicle frame apart at such speeds and jolting him hard, which only increased the rate at which he was bleeding out.

He saw a line rising out of the grass and parallel to the road. It was the edge of a railroad track, and Bolan could barely make out where it crossed the road about a quarter mile ahead. He placed the rifle sling between his teeth and quickly used the knife to slice the nylon belt off at the muzzle and shoulder butt sling attachment points.

Bolan turned the boot knife point down and stabbed it into the seat. Gritting his teeth he lifted his wounded leg and slid the nylon strap under it. He pulled the sling up, then quickly tied a knot in it about four inches above his gunshot wound.

The wheel jolted hard under his hand and he looked up. He released his tourniquet, grabbed the steering wheel with both hands and fought the Land Rover back onto the road. He climbed the slight incline and used the emergency brake to swing the Land Rover onto the train track. The wheels immediately began to pound with a harsh, undulating rhythm as he raced over the wooden railroad ties.

Though the shaking was even more brutal than that of the washed-out road, Bolan knew his chances of losing control had dramatically decreased. All he had to do was keep the SUV between the metal rails. The Executioner used his wounded right leg to work the gas and then propped his left knee against the steering wheel. With both hands free he continued worked frantically to finish tying the tourniquet into place before he bled to death. He laid the handle of the knife in the center of the knot he had secured above his wound and tied a second knot directly over the handle.

Bolan grabbed the blade by the center and began to twist the boot knife in 360-degree loops, cranking the nylon belt wrapped around his leg tighter and tighter. By the fifth turn his wound had stopped bleeding, and Bolan tied off the flat of the blade against his leg with the extra length of sling.

The vibrations from the railroad ties shivered up through his body in a staccato beat, and the pain it caused made him dizzy. He would start to fade and the rubber of his SUV tires would chafe against the steel rail of the track and jerk his attention back to reality.

The rain was omnipresent. In his shell-shocked state Bolan couldn't remember a time without the rain. He could see the headlights in his rearview mirror and knew the two pursuing vehicles were still behind him.

He dug out the cell phone and opened it. It continued to read No Signal. He put the phone away, too tired and wounded to be upset. He couldn't stay on the track forever, had known that even before he'd mounted the rails. Desperate times called for desperate measures, and Bolan had also known that fact for a long time, but that didn't really change the maneuver from being what it was—a simple stalling tactic.

The railroad tracks headed south and sooner or later, as close as he was to the border, Bolan knew he would run into a Burkina customs station. He was quickly running out of options. He felt woozy, sleepy. He realized he had to have lost more blood than he'd first thought. He tightened his grip on the steering wheel and forced himself to remain alert.

Bolan's mind raced, pulling up options, then discarding them just as quickly. There would be no help coming from Jack Grimaldi. The ace pilot would have risked heaven and earth to come to Bolan's side, but the rain simply made that impossible. It was always possible to fly an aircraft in bad weather, but odds had to be acknowledged and any chance of avoiding a crash under such conditions was minimal at best.

The question was moot anyway. If he couldn't even get a cell phone call out, there was no way Grimaldi was bringing a bird of any sort in. Bolan was trapped, battered and bleeding in a war zone without ally or aid and time was running out. He'd pushed his body to the very edge of its capabilities and he was living on borrowed time.

Bolan made his decision.

He looked to either side of him and saw the sheer grade of the banks dropping away from the edges of the train track.

Any attempt to pull off the tracks at too high a speed would lead to a rollover. Bolan checked his rearview mirror. The two Land Rovers behind him were pushing the chase and had closed to within fifty yards. That was point-blank range for a long rifle, and only the incessant jarring of the vehicle wheels on the railroad ties had kept their shots wild so far.

Bolan shifted his foot off the gas and pinned the steering wheel with his left knee. He didn't touch the brakes, in order to avoid shining the brake lights that could alert his pursuers to his intentions. Instead, he pulled the emergency brake and sent the Land Rover into a headfirst power slide.

The tires butted up against the iron railroad tracks violently, but the vehicle kept in its groove. Bolan snatched the AKM from the seat and twisted around, placing it across the seat rest. His rear windshield had already been blown out, and he was sheltered from the falling rain by the roof of the SUV.

He laid his sights on the vehicle careening toward him. Bolan was first and foremost a sniper.

He began to fire with a systematic and precise carnage. The rifle recoil into his shoulder was like the reassuring hand of an old friend. In that moment on the track, trapped in the vehicle between the rails, the Executioner came alive.

Bolan blew out the windshield on the lead chase vehicle and placed his second round into the driver of the speeding SUV. The driver's head jerked, and he slumped forward and slid down against the steering wheel until the vehicle's horn began to blare. The SUV continued rushing toward Bolan's now immobile vehicle.

The warrior shifted the AKM. At thirty yards the range was ridiculous for a man of Bolan's capabilities. He saw Le Crème scrambling for the steering wheel, desperate to bring the racing vehicle under control.

Bolan put a round through Le Crème's round face. The man's head snapped like a whip popping, and the top of his skull detached and flew into the back of the vehicle. Bolan shifted his weapon an almost imperceptible degree and fired another round through Le Crème's seat at twenty yards.

Du Toit was already scrambling. The 7.62 mm round punched through the center of Le Crème's seat and struck the man in his right arm as he threw himself down to the floor of the vehicle.

Bolan turned and rolled out of his Land Rover just as the second vehicle struck it. He gasped in surprise at the intensity of the pain as his injured leg struck the ground. He gave in to the pull of gravity and rolled down the bank, spilling gravel wildly.

Le Crème's Land Rover struck the back of Bolan's vehicle with a crash like thunder. Headlights turned on against the gloomy rain exploded in a shower of sparks. The front and back ends of each respective vehicle collapsed like aluminum cans, crumpling inward under the force. The dead gendarme driver catapulted through the windshield to sprawl across the crumpled hood of his vehicle.

The Land Rover directly behind Le Crème's remained unaware of the rapidly unfolding events and raced forward. As Bolan looked up from the bottom of the embankment, he saw the driver, a white South African mercenary, twist the wheel in a desperate attempt to avoid the pileup.

The speeding SUV left the train tracks going much too fast for the terrain. The front end of the vehicle popped up as it crashed over the rail. The Land Rover bounced down hard and began to slide over the edge of the bank. The driver gunned it and his vehicle started to slide further out of control.

The panicked driver overcorrected and the vehicle continued to pitch. Bolan watched the Land Rover begin its tip, his hyperstimulated senses making it seem as if the action were unfolding in slow motion. He saw the men in the vehicle cursing as they were thrown around inside the cab.

The second Land Rover rolled over in an awkward somersault of crunching metal and shattering glass. The vehicle rolled again and cleared the railroad bank, spinning out into the elephant grass. After rolling twice more the vehicle came to a rest on its roof with exploded tires spinning madly.

Bolan lifted himself on his good knee and pulled his salvaged rifle to him. He swept up the AKM and poured a long stream of gunfire into the wrecked SUV.

He tried and failed to ignite the second Land Rover's gas

tank as he had back on the edge of Yendere. He shot until his weapon locked on empty and then cast it aside. He looked down. His tourniquet had come loose during his fall and his leg was bleeding again.

He picked up the AKM and jammed the muzzle into the ground, using the assault rifle as a makeshift crutch. Bolan staggered to his feet. How much could he take? How far could he go? He wanted to lie down and sleep. He had faced too much, undergone too much. It would be easy to lie down. How many could have survived what he had already?

No, he thought suddenly. Why ask why? The intellectuals had hijacked the process. It wasn't important to question everything, it was important to understand that some things simply needed to be done.

Bolan drew his Beretta. The Executioner crouched in the rain ready for what was to happen next, anticipating it like a bullfighter or a snake charmer, waiting for that moment when the big show would turn on him with its own deadly intensity.

Du Toit came out of the back of the Land Rover with his submachine gun blazing. The Kalashnikov filled his hands. Bolan's bullets had hurt him badly and as he died he wanted only one thing—vengeance.

In the dark and the rain, each with their ears abused by the cacophony of weapons fire, the two men faced each other. Du Toit owned the high ground and in that moment wielded both the advantage of aggressive momentum and the ace card of superior firepower.

Du Toit unleashed the firepower of his AK-104. The 7.62 mm rounds stuttered out of his gun with mechanical intensity. Confused and hurt, bleeding and wounded, du Toit had been reduced to his animal state, striking out in a blind rage at the man who'd brought about his demise.

Bolan gave as good as he got.

He replied to du Toit's salvo with cool, meticulous accuracy, sweeping up the Beretta 93-R and unleashing a torrent of 3-round bursts. His accuracy with a pistol in combat was uncanny, unparalleled and ruthless.

The South African mercenary took the rounds, absorbing them like a sponge. He took a 9 mm Parabellum round in the belly and dropped to his knees, still firing. He felt bullets destroying the bones of his arm until it was impossible for him to hold his blazing weapon. Then the soft-nosed bullets smashed through his throat, and du Toit felt the precious gift of oxygen flee him like an unfaithful lover.

He went down hard. The Kalashnikov tumbled from fingers turned to liquid. The unforgiving rock of the railroad embankment reached up and slapped him. His head snapped forward and bounced off the rocks while the crimson nectar of his blood poured across the gray and white stones of the bank.

He rolled to his back and lifted his arms into the rain, but death was an elusive partner in du Toit's final dance. He tried to gasp and inhaled only his own blood. Coughing, he rolled his eyes and saw his enemy sag into the tall grass, as exhausted as he was.

Du Toit's fingers scratched for the pistol grip of his weapon as he saw his enemy falter. He felt a cold black rushing in to smother his vision.

Bolan lifted the Beretta once again. He sighted down the barrel and past the odd-sized shape of the cylinder that formed the Beretta's sound suppressor. He saw du Toit scratching haplessly at the ground, his weapon beyond reach.

A smile tugged at the corner of Bolan's mouth as he sighted his weapon in. I do not judge them, he thought, their actions judge them. I am their judgment.

Bolan pulled the trigger.

23

The Executioner lowered his pistol and looked down at his leg. His pants were soaked with blood. He looped the ends of his tourniquet back into place and patiently secured them again. Once the bleeding had stopped he began to apply a pressure dressing he'd made using his outer shirt. He folded up a mass of elephant grass and sandwiched that in between folds of his cut-up shirt before securing the bandage over his wound and loosening his tourniquet. Bolan forced himself to his feet when he was done, using the empty AKM as a crutch.

Despite the stifling humidity and relentless heat he felt chilled. He looked around him and saw the landscape was broken only by the industrial scar of the railroad. The track ran from north to south, and Bolan knew he was now closer to Burkina Faso's border with the Ivory Coast than to any town.

He needed medical attention, or at the very least medical supplies. If La Crème had been in contact with any other government forces, which seemed likely, Bolan knew he was a wanted man. His safest bet was to make it across the border and perhaps tell Ivory Coast forces that he had been innocently caught up in the fighting.

Bolan forced himself to start moving. His head ached from the abuse he had suffered and from the effects of dehydration.

He used the break in the tall grass close to the railway embankment to maneuver across the rough terrain. He leaned heavily on the butt of his rifle as he pushed his way forward.

He walked for an hour and then the rain stopped. He looked up and it seemed that the cloud cover wasn't quite as low as it had been.

Bolan stopped walking. He didn't sit to rest because he feared that if he lowered himself to the ground he'd never be able to lift himself up again. Already the muscles of his hips and legs were cramping.

He pulled out Saragossa's cell phone. He felt like a gambler in Vegas about to pull the handle on a slot machine just one more time. He opened the phone. Despite himself, he felt the corners of his mouth lift in relief.

He could get a single bar, but that should be enough. Saragossa's phone had enough of a signal to transmit. Bolan used his grimy, blood-crusted thumb to scroll through the options on the phone menu. He found the picture of Saragossa's notes and prepped the device to send the picture to another user.

Bolan tapped in the number to Grimaldi's phone from memory and pushed the Send button. The screen went black, then showed the data uploading in the form of a growing bar graph. A positive message flashed. He watched the screen intently for a couple of minutes to ensure the picture didn't bounce back due to atmospheric interference as it had before.

Bolan hit the End button, then folded the phone. He slipped it into his pocket in case the team at Stony Man Farm could retrieve any more useful intelligence from it later. Bolan took out his sat phone and hit the speed dial.

"Goddamn, Sarge!" Grimaldi yelled into the phone.

"Jack, check your personal phone. You have it with you, right?" Bolan said quickly.

"Yep." The pilot was silent for a long moment. "You sent me a photo. I've got it."

"Good, send it on to Bear and Hal. Make sure they get it."

"Consider it done. Listen, Sarge, Bear is feeding me situation reports. The cease-fire is in effect. There has been a ton of chatter about a tall white man shooting everyone to shit."

"It's nice to be appreciated," Bolan said.

"Christ, Sarge, you don't sound so good."

"I could use a nap," Bolan admitted.

He began to walk again, wincing with each step. The constant moisture had caused blisters to form on his feet, and each step was intensely painful. Bolan looked up and decided the clouds definitely seemed less dense above his head.

"Listen, buddy," Grimaldi continued, "the Burkina authorities are plenty upset. They accused the Ivory Coast of using hired mercenaries, which they denied. As part of the cease-fire agreement arranged by the African Union, the Ivory Coast has agreed to turn you over if their forces find you."

"Find me?"

"Well, any white man in the Yendere border region will be taken into custody until their identity as a noncombatant can be verified."

"That's a little extreme."

"I'll lodge a complaint. But the point is, your pickup is going to have to be hot. There is no refuge in the region for you."

"Jack, I haven't got a lot of hiking left in me right now," Bolan said.

Grimaldi paused. It was as close to an admission of weakness that the pilot had ever heard from the big warrior. On the other end of the signal Grimaldi felt his heart beat faster.

"Do you know where you are? Do you have your GPS or any navigational equipment?"

"No. I lost my pack after the drop," Bolan replied. "The roads around here are going to be crawling with Burkina forces and the whole damn country is socked in with the rain."

"You let me do the flying, Sarge. Do you have any idea where you are?"

"Roughly. I'm east of the rail line just outside Yendere, about five miles north of the border with the Ivory Coast," Bolan replied.

"Just a second," Grimaldi said. "Let me look at the maps I have here."

Bolan continued to walk, keeping the railroad to his right. Every step he took was pulling him closer to the border and to more danger. Even though Bolan knew that, it seemed wiser to continue traveling in that direction than any other under the circumstances.

"Sarge, you still there?" Grimaldi asked.

"I'm here."

"I've got NSA images taken of the region just before the rains hit. I'm marrying those up with U.S. Army land maps of the area. I've also got a complete workup on the area from some officer in the National Reconnaissance Office. I think I've got a plan—but it's a tough one."

Bolan looked down at his bandaged leg. Blood had completely soaked the dressing. "Go ahead," he said.

"Have you crossed a dirt road since you left the rail line? Maybe more of a trail, really."

"No, not yet."

"Go south until you hit that. Follow it east until it runs into the Petite Comoc. Hug the bank and follow the river southeast. The Petite Comoe feeds the Komoe River."

"The Komoe is thirty miles from here. I won't make it that far," Bolan said.

"You won't have to, Sarge. The NRO's report says there is an old mining operation on the Petite, run by a mining company out of Nova Scotia. It was abandoned a few years ago."

"Why follow this dirt track then?" Bolan asked. "Shouldn't there be a rail link to a mining operation?"

"Nope, no rail link, not even a good secondary road." Grimaldi sounded excited. "Heavy materials were shipped to the site by river barge, and what little gold they did find was shipped out the same way. But here's the important part, Sarge. The personnel, the engineers and administration types used seaplanes to get in and out."

"Seaplanes?"

"That's right. If you can make it to the abandoned site, there'll be a dock. I'll land a plane on the river and get you out."

"In this weather? Do you even have a plane with pontoons where you are?" Bolan asked.

"I told you, Sarge. You let me worry about the flying. It looks like it's about eight miles. Can you make it?"

"I'll make it. But a place like that, out of the way but with modern buildings, won't there be squatters?"

"There's no information on that. It's on the border, Sarge. Drug runners could use the site, the MPCI elements could have taken it over. Hell, a clan of goat herders could be living there. We just don't know."

"I'll get there," the Executioner said.

"I'll make this happen, Sarge."

"I know you will," Bolan said.

The big warrior hesitated. He didn't want to worry his friend, but it was foolish to allow pride to overrule common sense.

"Jack," Bolan said, "if you can swing it, I'm going to need some medical supplies. More than a first-aid kit. IV fluids, plasma if you can get it and antibiotics."

"Christ, Sarge—"

"I'll be there, at the mining compound. Do what you can. I'll call you once I've seen the place, let you know what the situation on the ground is."

"I'll be there, I swear it," the pilot said.

Grimaldi cut his connection with Bolan and immediately began working. He had set up his support operation for Bolan in Bamako, the capital city of Mali. While China remained its largest export partner, U.S. Army Special Forces had been heavily involved in training Mali army units and, as a result, diplomatic ties had improved to the point that U.S. intelligence agencies had established small logistics stations there.

Grimaldi and Bolan had entered the West Africa area of operations with the necessary clearances and code words allowing them to tap into the assets of other U.S. agencies already in place.

Grimaldi had access to a number of planes at the Bamako International Airport, the use of a small safehouse near the runways, complete with secured communications equipment, and contact numbers for U.S. Army intelligence officers in the area as well as the CIA case officer at the consulate.

The pilot did not immediately call these points of contact. He did not have time to waste on official channels. He needed to get in touch with someone who could *make* things happen—someone who would move heaven and earth to help the asset known as Striker.

Grimaldi called Barbara Price.

In a tense voice Grimaldi explained Bolan's situation in the field and his own scat-of-the-pants plan to exfiltrate the big man.

"That's not exactly the most detailed operational plan I've ever heard, even for you." Price's voice was tight but she kept herself pragmatic.

"I'm doing my best," Grimaldi replied.

"I'm having Bear transfer the funds now. Take down this number. It's to a slush account the Company uses to facilitate local activities. I still don't know what you're going to do if you don't find someone willing to do it."

"That isn't an option, Barb. I owe him my life," the pilot replied.

"I understand. Be careful and keep me informed," Price said.

"I'm on it," Grimaldi promised.

GRIMALDI IGNORED THE RAIN as he left the taxi. He wore a lightweight windbreaker and a battered ball cap. He'd taken a Beretta 92 from the wall safe of the covert station house and kept it tucked into the waistband at the back of his jeans. In a briefcase, along with ten thousand euros, Grimaldi carried a manila envelope containing a variable interest bond made out to Adrir Lejeune. Former FBI agent and Stony Man Farm computer wizard, Carmen Delahunt, had been able to identify the Algerian ex-pat as a potential source even with the short notice Grimaldi's request had given.

Adrir Lejeune was the son of a French national father and an Algerian mother. Sixty-five years old, he had retired from running a modestly successful air freight company. The man kept a small villa and a Cessna airplane outfitted with pontoons on the Niger River in an upscale suburb of Bamako.

Grimaldi could see the plane as he approached the walk leading to the man's villa. The Cessna was moored next to a dock leading off the back deck of Lejeune's house. It floated easily on the flat, slow-moving current of the river. From what Grimaldi could see the plane looked like it was in immaculate condition.

Grimaldi opened the gate in the wrought-iron fence running around the villa. A little flower garden and date trees had been cultivated along the walk, and with the rain Lejeune's plants were in full bloom. Grimaldi walked up to the door and knocked. Inside a dog began to bark.

The dog sounded big. A male voice cursed in French and then laughed. The dog fell silent. After a moment Grimaldi could hear the locks in the door being snapped back. He could also hear the dog growling low in its chest, like the rumble of a diesel engine.

The front door swung open and Grimaldi found himself confronted by an exotic sight. The man before him was tall, almost six and half feet, and whipcord thin with a wild mane of silver hair and a black eye patch. As startling as the man's appearance was, it paled in comparison to the dog that stood at his side.

The Rhodesian ridgeback, known as the African lion hound, stood over two feet high at the withers and weighed about ninety pounds. The distinctive ridge of fur running along the animal's muscular back stood out in vivid relief. The dog sized Grimaldi up and showed the pilot its fangs.

"Oui?" the man asked. "Do I know you?"

"Um, do you speak English?"

"A little bit," Lejeune replied. "How about…what the hell do you want?"

The tall man did not calm his dog or offer to let Grimaldi come into the house out of the rain. The man's demeanor did little to bolster Grimaldi's hopes for a quick, complication-free transaction.

To hell with it, Grimaldi thought. I never was a snake oil salesman, I'll just throw the money in his face and see if he bites.

"Look, I know this is your day off, I know you're retired. I know you don't care. I need a pontoon kit, I need it put on and I need it done an hour ago. Or I need your plane."

The man was already shaking his head as Grimaldi rushed on.

"Listen to me. I am willing to pay you for your trouble. By pay you I mean twice the price of materials, twice the rate for labor and ten thousand in cash, right now, for your help. Or double the value of that Cessna sitting out on the dock. Your choice, boss."

Lejeune looked at Grimaldi, clearly stunned by his declaration. Grimaldi, sensing he was close to sealing the deal, handed the man his briefcase. Lejeune took the case and looked inside. He looked up at Grimaldi. His single eye narrowed in suspicion, then the deep creases on his face relaxed and Lejeune smiled, showing big white teeth.

"Let's do it," he said.

GRIMALDI WAS IN THE AIR and flying fast above the cloud cover. The clouds hugged the earth, thick and dark with pent-up humidity. He checked his flight instruments carefully, but he knew that when it came time to descend into the roiling mass below they would be of little help.

Adrir Lejeune had proved himself to be a professional. When presented with the payments he had delivered his services to his customer with speed and skill. Grimaldi could only pray that the rest of the plan he'd thrown together would unfold just as smoothly as the first part.

The Stony Man cybernetics team headed by Aaron Kurtzman had utilized Hal Brognola's contacts in the Justice Department to concoct a tight plan based on current U.S. government operations in the nearby country of Ghana.

Ghana shared a border with Burkina Faso. It was a major illicit producer of cannabis and an important hub in the international transfer of both southwestern and southeastern Asian heroin traffic. Of late it had become a spoke on the South America to Europe cocaine shipment points.

To combat this, and the ties of narcoterrorists to larger geopolitical terror networks, the Drug Enforcement Administration, supported by a CIA UAV drone team and a communications-encryption officer, had set up a field base in the northwestern part of Ghana, along the Black Volta River in the city of Wa.

Once Grimaldi had the wounded Bolan on board he would turn the nose of the Cessna east-by-southeast and run like hell right into the teeth of the rainstorm. The plan was last minute, at the limits of their resources and daring to the point of desperation.

With a little luck, Grimaldi thought it might even work.

BOLAN LAY HIDDEN in the tall grass.

The pain in his leg was an agony. He lifted his head and looked down. The wound was badly infected. Scarlet streaks ran up and down his thigh in trailers of poison. The infection around the open area had begun to stink, and Bolan was afraid that gangrene would set in too strongly to be reversed.

His body was hot with fever, and he shook often with the chills. The rain had started to fall again, incessant as ever, and he cursed it. If there had been no rain, there would be flies and the maggots of flies would eat the necrotic flesh around his wound, ingesting the infection. But there were no flies because the rain fell too hard.

The hike had been brutal. The constant movement pulled the clotting scabs inside his wound loose, and he began to leak blood. He retied the bandages, but his materials were so poor it made little difference.

He was afraid of the chills that would sweep down over him

and grip him in fierce, but mercifully brief spells. If it was malaria, he knew he'd die. The disease would kill him in his already dehydrated and weakened state.

Bolan dragged his broken body and almost useless leg across eight miles of African bush. By the time he saw the river for the first time his vision was so blurry it was as if he were looking at the world through the prism of cataracts. His tongue had swollen in his mouth, and he had trouble swallowing properly.

Once, he became so exhausted that he had been forced to sit before he fell over. But the acacia tree he chose for shelter had been the home of fire ants and he had snapped out of his daze in pain as the insects were driven to a frenzy by the rich smell of his seeping blood. With no canteen water to flush his wound Bolan had been forced to cut away his pant leg and expose the vicious, crawling ants to the force of the rain.

It was during that time that he saw how far and deep the infection had spread. The idea that he wouldn't make it was something he could quantify and even accept. And he wasn't ready to give up his struggle, his War Everlasting.

He thought of Aaron Kurtzman, whose indomitable will had seen the man through the loss of the use of his legs. Bolan tried to imagine himself confined to Stony Man while Able Team and Phoenix Force deployed out to fight. He felt ashes fill his mouth at the thought. He tried to swallow the bitter taste away but found he couldn't.

Then he got up and walked some more.

The rain never stopped falling and Bolan was so dizzy from fever and his leg so useless, that he was forced to crawl the last mile. During that labor he realized he'd stopped sweating and knew that was a very bad sign. Sometime later he found the abandoned mining site Grimaldi had described. An ancient barge was tied to a dock made of wood rapidly disintegrating from neglect in the overpowering heat and constant humidity.

The river in front of the dock ran for about two football fields, deep and slow. Beyond the edges of the nearly stagnant minilake, the arc of the river narrowed and twisted so sharply that a plane couldn't have landed there. If Grimaldi was going to land it would have to be directly in front of the compound dock.

That would have been fine if the gunmen hadn't held the area.

Bolan couldn't tell who they were, whether a splinter faction of the MPCI or simply a criminal group that had stumbled upon a conveniently remote and ready-made base of operations. But who they were didn't matter to Bolan. Every man with a gun in the region was simply a man ready to kill him. To pretend otherwise was naive folly. More than likely the group was locals hired to do grunt labor or provide security for the mine and had simply moved into the built-up area after the company had pulled out.

Bolan crawled through the elephant grass and surveyed the camp. He tried to focus his feverish thoughts and ignore the throbbing of his rotting leg. He forced his mind to keep busy, to organize and catalog the threat he saw on the riverbank. The compound was rough but prefabricated.

Shaped like a K, the buildings included three double-wide mobile homes obviously intended for offices and as the barracks for company officers. Cinder-block buildings had been used for bunkhouses to billet a small cadre of miners. Beyond that there was a roofed motor pool, a process plant and a shabby looking company cantina. All the buildings were spaced around a slash-and-burn clearing about five acres in size.

Bolan saw men dressed in civilian clothes and military

uniforms moving between the buildings. They were armed with AKMs and RPK machine guns. One battered pickup truck had a 75 mm recoilless rifle mounted in the back. As bad as that development was, Bolan was more worried about a pile of long, empty boxes he saw piled behind one of the mobile homes. They looked very much like the packing crates for old Soviet SA-7 Grail man-portable antiaircraft missiles.

Near Bolan a red pickup sat rusting on soft tires. The truck bed had been removed and replaced with a wider, flatbed platform made out of cutdown railroad ties. It had obviously served as a general purpose mule around the site for decades. A massive, industrial toolbox had been fitted onto the bed at the back of the cab. The metal container was dented and the faded red paint was chipped and peeling.

Inside the truck two young gunmen on sentry duty smoked marijuana and listened to music coming from a battered old radio kept together by silver duct tape.

Bolan watched them with bloodshot eyes. From somewhere behind the processing plant he heard sheep bleating.

He thought about Grimaldi trying to land a plane in the tropical downpour. He thought about the gunmen unloading with machine guns and rockets on a thin-skinned civilian aircraft. He thought about himself trying to make it across an acre of open ground, onto the dock, and into Grimaldi's sitting duck with one leg and no long weapon.

Bolan almost laughed out loud. He would never say die. But his hopes rested on putting one of his oldest and closest friends into suicidal danger. He couldn't ask Grimaldi to try such an impossible stunt. He couldn't ask because he knew his old friend would do it.

Bolan lowered his head, tired. It had been a good run. His battle may have been eternal, but the Executioner knew he was not and he had made peace with that, as with many unpleasant facts, a long time ago. Thirty minutes earlier Grimaldi had called to report that he was flying above the cloud ceiling and was ready to roll on Bolan's word.

The warrior hadn't seen the condition of the camp by that time, but now he had. There was no way he was exposing his friend to this. Bolan closed his eyes for a second to gather his strength. His head sagged against the crook of his arm.

He snapped awake. He didn't know how long he'd been out, and fought to drive the cobwebs from his brain. Was that the same song playing in the cab of the truck? He thought it was but he couldn't be sure. He reached down and pulled his sat phone free. White spittle gathered at the corners of his mouth, and his lips were swollen and cracked. He tried to softly clear the tightness out of his throat and found he could barely swallow.

He pressed Grimaldi's number on his speed dial with a grimy thumb.

"Sarge! Go ahead, you ready?"

Bolan tried to answer and all that came out was a weak croak.

"Sarge! Are you there?" Grimaldi's voice was frantic.

Dimly Bolan worried that the pilot was talking so loud the guards in the truck would hear him. He tried to speak again, but his voice came out too soft and strangled.

"Goddamn it, Sarge!" Grimaldi snarled. "Are you there, buddy? Are you okay?"

Bolan forced himself to swallow hard. His throat burned with a raw, red pain but he found his voice.

"Abort," he managed.

"Abort? What the hell are you talking about?"

"Abort, I'm on-site. Hostiles control the LZ."

"Christ, Sarge, I can barely understand you. Are you hit?"

"Not important. They have SA-7s. You have no chance."

"Then pull-out and head south down the river two miles. I'll land there," the pilot replied.

"Jack, abort, I won't make it two miles."

"Christ," Grimaldi repeated. "How bad are you hit?".

"That's not important. The LZ is a no go. Abort."

There was a moment of silence and Bolan felt hope swell in him. Maybe he had convinced Grimaldi that it was impossible. Bolan felt his eyes closing.

"I'm bringing the plane in now, Sarge," Grimaldi said. "Get your ass in the water, now."

"Jack, no!" Bolan said. "They'll blow you out of the water!"

"I can't copy, Sarge," Grimaldi said. "I'm breaking contact now, be in the water. I repeat—be in the water."

The line went dead and Bolan grabbed the sat phone tightly in one fist. He despised not being in control. He felt a shuddering chill shake his body and forced himself up onto his good knee.

He had to make it to the water. Grimaldi would sit there and be shot to pieces waiting for him. If the Executioner wanted to save his friend, there was nothing more he could do other than what Grimaldi had instructed.

Bolan looked up into the sky but could see nothing because of the falling rain. The visibility was terrible, but at least there were no winds. An amphibious landing under such conditions was hard enough, even for a pilot as experienced as Jack Grimaldi, but if there had been severe winds it would have been impossible.

Bolan pushed himself to a standing position. His hand pulled the Beretta 93-R from his shoulder holster. It wasn't just that the 9 mm pistol was silenced, Bolan didn't think he was strong enough in his condition to handle the recoil of his Desert Eagle.

The warrior staggered forward. His eyes crossed and the truck appeared in a blurry double image. He forced himself forward, stretching out a hand to find the wooden bed of the truck. His hand shook like an alcoholic in detox.

Bolan slipped and was forced to use his bad leg to try to keep from going down. Pain racked his body and he almost moaned out loud. He stumbled and tried to regain his balance, but he was dizzy from his fever.

He fell and struck the muddy ground and filthy puddles of rainwater splashed over him. He looked up to see if the guards in the pickup had been alerted. He heard their music. In the sideview mirror he saw the guard in the driver seat inhale a lungful of smoke.

Bolan pushed himself onto his good knee and used his free hand to pull himself forward. He dragged the Beretta through the muddy puddle and held it ready. He reached the back of the truck. With one hand Bolan grabbed the edge and hauled himself up. The weight of his two hundred plus pounds tilted the truck on its suspension.

Bolan worked himself to his feet. His movements were so slow they seemed exaggerated, even to himself. He gritted his teeth as the movement ripped fresh clots from his infected wound, and he felt the hot splash of his own blood running down his leg once more. Dimly he wondered just how much blood he had left, since he seemed to have lost so much of it already.

Bolan looked up but the angle was wrong and he couldn't see the guard's reflection in the vehicle mirror. He leaned a hip against the truck bed and reached out with his good hand. Once he was leaning forward he took a step. Bolan repeated the awkward procedure twice more as he made his torturous way down the length of the old pickup truck.

The rain cutting into him seemed hard enough to drive him to his knees, and Bolan knew that without the support of the truck bed he would have fallen. He reached a hand out and leaned against the roof of the cab. His felt like vomiting, and there was a ringing in his ears. His shaking hand came down on a buildup of moisture and slid out from underneath him.

Bolan fell forward and grunted as his chest struck the corner of the pickup cab. He staggered back. He heard a shout of surprise come from inside the truck. He felt a sudden tightness in his chest, like a fist squeezing his heart. A mild electrical jolt passed through his left shoulder and down his arm.

He looked up, blinking away the blurriness. The driver's door was thrown open, and the guard bailed out of the cab. Bolan couldn't catch his breath and he gulped for air. The driver put one foot on the muddy ground and brought his ancient AK-47 around.

Bolan shot him before the man could fire.

The man's head snapped to the side and blood ran like drool from a fissure in his temple. The guard tumbled out of the truck cab and landed in a heap at Bolan's feet. The warrior fell forward and caught himself on the open door. He leaned into the cab and was almost overpowered by the smell of pungent smoke. He saw the other sentry aiming at him and the Beretta coughed twice.

The rounds hit the gunman in the chest. The man triggered a burst from his AK-47 and rolled onto the ground, dead or paralyzed.

Bolan sagged against the open door. The pressure in his chest there had been replaced by a dull ache. His heart was beating hard to make up for the loss of blood, attempting to circulate the oxygen his cells craved by working harder. But as he lost blood he was writing checks he couldn't cash, forcing himself into shock. He waited to see if the pain in his chest would worsen or abate. It seemed to be doing neither, and he let himself fall over into the cab of the truck.

Bolan dropped the Beretta onto the seat and reached for the keys dangling in the ignition. He put his wounded leg on the gas and turned the key in the ignition.

Behind him the radio fell silent as the track ended and he heard men shouting as if from across a vast gulf. Now I'm in for it, he thought. He leaned back against the seat and let his head rock loosely as he pushed down on the gas. The pain in his chest was sharper, more urgent. Dully he heard the truck engine race and realized he wasn't in drive.

He grabbed the gearshift where it stuck out of the steering column and manhandled it into gear. He heard weapons fire as the truck began rolling forward. The engine kept racing and the car lurching as the rpm cycled up. He looked down and saw that he had put the truck's transmission into second gear by mistake. Behind him another song began to blare out of the stereo.

He didn't feel strong enough to change the gear. He looked over to the passenger side of the vehicle. The door hung open and he noticed with a detached sense of reality that the guard he'd shot had his foot caught and was being dragged through the mud beside the rolling pickup.

He heard the chatter of weapons fire over the music and saw sparks flash off the engine hood. From the upper corner of his windshield he saw Grimaldi bringing the Cessna plane in over the treetops along the riverbank.

"Crazy man," he muttered.

His windshield shattered and rounds struck the seat beside

him. Stuffing exploded into the air and floated down through the rain. Bolan fought to breathe.

The rain struck the flat brown spread of the slow-moving river, causing an unending series of splashes and ripples. Bolan watched Grimaldi drop the plane right onto the river and was finally able to hear the roar of the plane's engine for the first time.

He slapped ineffectually at the steering wheel, trying to keep the truck pointed toward the squat little dock. A teenager in a black T-shirt and filthy khaki shorts leaped in front of the sputtering pickup and began firing an assault rifle. Bolan saw green tracer fire arc into the truck and steam billowed up around the edges of the engine hood. More of the windshield was blown away, and Bolan felt shards of glass sting his already lacerated face. A bullet struck the stereo and silenced the music as it exploded and fell onto the seat.

He could feel the vibration of the rounds striking the vehicle, but somehow the little workhorse simply kept rolling forward. More out of habit than a sense of survival, Bolan picked up the Beretta and fired through the open windshield. His aim was lazy and he had no idea where the bullets went.

The return fire seemed to rattle the gunman as much as the fact that the battered old vehicle continued to move. The teenager leaped out of the way as Bolan rolled past. The corner of the cab above his head rang as 7.62 mm slugs perforated the structure.

Bolan didn't hear the sound; he was working too hard to breathe, to stay awake. Out on the river Grimaldi had turned the plane around and was coming toward the dock. The pontoons churned up white froth on the dirty water as the ace pilot powered in. Bolan had a dim impression of the heavy stutter of a crew-served weapon opening up.

The pickup jolted under him as he left the muddy field and rolled onto the wooden planks of the dock. The rear windshield exploded behind him. Clutching his chest, Bolan tried to lean forward but found he was too weak and couldn't rise. The industrial toolbox directly behind the cab soaked up bullets in a horrific, rattling din.

The truck sputtered along the dock, and Bolan managed to slide over until he leaned up against the driver's door and it swung open under his weight. He looked down and saw the greasy wood of the pier racing past. He looked up and saw Grimaldi's plane slide in front of the dock. He jerked the truck's steering wheel and drove the pickup off the dock to the right.

He had a sense of flying and saw the weathered, mildewed wood under the truck disappear to be replaced by the brown water of the river. The nose of the truck struck the surface of the water, and the jolt shoved Bolan up against the steering wheel. Water rushed in warm and fetid through the broken windows and open doors.

Bolan tumbled out of the sinking vehicle and into the sluggish current of the river. The pain in his chest was excruciating and radiated through his body into the muscles of his back. The water closed over his head, and Bolan kicked out for the surface.

The Executioner clawed for the surface with frantic strokes of his arms. His wounded leg was an anchor dragging him down. He broke the surface and saw the pontoon of Grimaldi's plane.

He reached out for it, and it felt as if someone had slammed his hand with a ball peen hammer. Blood materialized and Bolan sucked in a mouthful of warm river water as he gasped at the sudden bullet wound. He sputtered. His hand hit the smooth plastic of the pontoon, and then he went under.

Suddenly he felt a strong hand grab his trailing arm, and his descent into the depths abruptly halted. Another hand joined the first and he felt himself being hauled toward the surface. His head broke through the water, and he blinked the filthy liquid out of his eyes.

He saw Jack Grimaldi standing above him on the pontoon. The light-skinned Cessna was all that stood between the two men and a virtual orgy of gunfire coming from the riverbank. Grimaldi strained to haul the Executioner out of the river. He was yelling something but Bolan couldn't hear him, could only see his face distort with the effort of what he was screaming.

Grimaldi put his arms around Bolan's torso and heaved him through the pilot's door. Bolan flopped across the seat and Grimaldi rudely shoved him over before climbing in after him and gunning the plane.

Bolan landed roughly on his side and realized he wasn't breathing. Then he realized he didn't care.

24

The inside of the cockpit was shot to hell. Was still *being* shot to hell. The cockpit of the Cessna sat high in relationship to the body and offered a 360-degree field of vision. Every single window in the airframe had been blown out or spiderwebbed by the impact of heavy-caliber bullets.

Rain lashed in through the open windows with a vengeance, soaking everything and leaving puddles on the floor. Bullets struck in almost identical volume. Grimaldi worked the controls of the revving plane and initiated his takeoff. Bullets pinged through the aircraft and shuddered seats in the back of the cabin with their impact.

"Stay down, Sarge!" Grimaldi yelled. "I'll get us off the water."

The pilot had seen how badly hurt Bolan was, and he didn't believe him capable of returning any kind of covering fire. Bolan had been white as a sheet from blood loss, and as soon as he had altitude Grimaldi would break open the Special Forces medic kit he had taken from the safehouse in Mali.

The Cessna began to skim along the surface of the river. A bullet struck the whirling rotor and sparks fanned up like fireworks, but the blades kept spinning. Grimaldi had no idea why the engine was still working as he could see bullets ripping holes in the compartment housing. He heard bullets whiz by his head as he hunched down. An RPG-7 rocket sailed across the nose of the plane and disappeared from Grimaldi's view before exploding.

He got to the end of the wide spot in the river and began to spin the plane around to start the final takeoff run. For every step of the way he would be exposed to withering enemy fire.

As Grimaldi powered the Cessna forward, he risked a glance at the riverbank and felt icy-squirts of fear splash into his stomach like frigid jolts. The bank was crawling with gunmen, infested like an ant hill, and each one wielded a weapon capable of bringing down the civilian aircraft.

As Grimaldi approached the takeoff, it seemed as if he were sailing the plane straight into a spiderweb of crisscrossing arcs of tracer fire. The clatter and rattle of lead penetrating the cab was loud enough to be heard over the driving rain coming in through the shattered windows.

Grimaldi pulled back on the yoke, forcing the plane up off the surface of the river as if by sheer willpower. As he began to lift the Cessna, something caught his eye and he turned to look despite the precariousness of his situation.

He saw a young gunman run up to the edge of the riverbank and drop to a knee. A dreadful feeling of helplessness rushed into Grimaldi despite his prodigious courage.

The gunman threw the SA-7b Grail rocket launcher to his shoulder and swept it around to sight in on the plane. Grimaldi knew the man-portable missile had a ceiling of 2300 yards and a kill range out to about 5500 yards. It used a passive IR guidance system and was utilized in a "tail-chase" capacity. The heat of the Cessna's engines would draw the deadly thing right to them.

"Sarge," Grimaldi shouted. "I need you, buddy!"

Grimaldi pulled the nose of the Cessna up over the trees along the riverbank, prop-clawing for open sky. He felt a shudder pass through the frame as the pontoons slammed their way through the topmost branches. The muscles on his forearms stood out like cables as he fought the yoke to keep his pitch even under the impact.

The pilot snapped his head around to look at Bolan and saw the ash gray tinge of his features, the slack muscles of his face and the fixed, dull stare of his eyes.

Jack Grimaldi had seen death many, many times before. He recognized the reaper when it looked at him and he saw death in his old friend's face.

"Oh, Jesus," he cursed.

Still holding back on the yoke, forcing the Cessna to climb, Grimaldi prayed he would reach a sufficient altitude quickly enough. He looked back over his shoulder and across the cab of the plane. Through the jagged glass of one of the broken rear windows he saw the flash of the missile launch.

Spewing dark smoke as it flew, the warhead spun in looping spirals as it buzzed through the rain toward the Cessna. In the thick humidity and falling water the exhaust of the airplane would shine like phosphorescence in the dark.

Grimaldi lurched to the side and reached under the copilot seat. He pulled the item secured in brackets free and sat up, one hand holding the stick of the plane steady in its climb.

He held an orange plastic breech-loaded 12-gauge flare gun. The Very pistol, as it was commonly called, fired a one-and-a-half-inch cartridge that when shot into the air burned intensely hot and bright as it moved along its arc of illumination.

Grimaldi swiveled in his seat and saw the missile round speeding toward the Cessna, outstripping the plane as he fought for altitude. Grimaldi knew the missile system had been imbedded with circuitry designed to make the missile resistant to chaff and flares dropped by aircraft in defense.

But he also knew that in reality those defensive measures were largely imperfect and could be exploited. Grimaldi stretched out of the pilot's seat and pushed the pistol through the broken side window of the airplane. He angled his weapon back toward the chasing missile and pulled the trigger. The 12-gauge round popped sharply and a red-tail flare sailed down the length of the battered Cessna toward the incoming missile.

The arc of the flare flashed with white-hot intensity as it passed the exhaust of the plane and tracked in front of the flying missile, catching the warhead's passive IR sensors in a siren call of heat and light.

The missile suddenly shifted its trajectory and zoomed after the brightly burning flare. Grimaldi banked the plane hard against the rain in the opposite direction. Behind him the missile warhead reached the end of its self-destruct fuse and exploded in a ball of fire.

Grimaldi barked out his laughter. He realized he'd cheated death one more time. The relief was tangible. But, as good as it was, the maneuver hadn't been enough by itself to ensure survival.

Fighting the rain, Grimaldi climbed the damaged plane into the low clouds over the African grasslands. Meteorological reports had put the rain clouds at almost the level of fog, hovering in tight to the nape of the earth at under three thousand feet.

As the plane soared upward, Grimaldi began to shiver. The temperature drop was noticeable and immediate. He knew if Bolan were to be saved he would have to put the plane on autopilot, a dangerous proposition in bad weather and at such a low altitude, even if the instrument worked properly.

Nearly frenzied, Grimaldi barked another short, harsh laugh at the thought. He set the controls and then scrambled out of his seat. The plane was a bullet-riddled wreck, and the stress of rain and rising altitude were real threats at the forefront of his mind.

The pilot stepped over Bolan's body where he was sprawled in the short aisle between cockpit and cabin. Moving fast he snatched up the medic kit he had acquired earlier in Bamako. He did not try to initiate CPR. It was unrealistic to think he could sustain CPR under such conditions if his old friend did not respond immediately.

What Grimaldi planned to do would either work or he would be burying the Executioner at Stony Man Farm.

25

The Stony Man pilot pushed Bolan flat on his back and drew the knife out of Bolan's boot sheath. He sliced open the T-shirt and exposed the white-gray flesh of Bolan's bruised chest.

The shirt was soaked from the rain and mud, splattered with blood to such a degree that it was impossible to tell what the original color had been. Bruises and dozens of lacerations dotted the Executioner's body as if a road map of abuse. A bullet had gouged a line of flesh along Bolan's side, leaving muscle exposed.

"Come on, Sarge," Grimaldi begged.

The pilot's hands shook as he worked the fasteners on the OD-green canvas bag. Special Forces medics were skilled to the training level of a physician's assistant, as well as being competent in veterinary medicine. The medic kit was as complete as a Red Cross clinic or a New York City ambulance, and the Stony Man pilot had the training to help his old friend.

Grimaldi spilled out bags of IV fluids, vials containing antibiotics, bandages, syringes of morphine, and splint-gear for broken bones, all the while clawing through the equipment for what he needed most. In a top flap pocket Grimaldi found what he was looking for—two filled syringes of epinephrine, the synthesized analog of adrenaline.

The pilot took a deep calming breath and his hands were steady as he grabbed both sturdy syringes and pulled off the caps with his teeth. He curled the index finger of his left hand around one syringe to secure it, then rested that hand against Bolan to steady his aim. Grimaldi grabbed the remaining syringe like a dart and thrust it down.

The long needle slipped between Bolan's ribs and jabbed into the left ventricle of Bolan's heart. Grimaldi pushed the plunger down and injected the drug straight into the cardiac muscle. When he was finished he pulled out the spike and tossed the used syringe aside.

Operating in a nearly frantic state, Grimaldi took the second needle and repeated the process. He pulled the second syringe clear and threw it aside as well, completely oblivious to protocols. He felt the plane suddenly lurch and then veer sharply underneath them as the autopilot system, possibly damaged by machine-gun fire, kicked off under the stress.

Grimaldi leaped to his feet and staggered toward the cockpit. He threw himself into his seat and began to wrestle with the controls. He fought to pull the light plane out of its spin, gripping the stick so tightly the veins in his hands and forearms stood out in vivid view under the stress.

"Come on, come on!" Grimaldi screamed.

Realizing he was never going to fight the momentum of the dropping roll, Grimaldi instead went with it. He pushed the flaps down and tightened the rotation, increasing the output of his engine thrust. The plane spun into a jerking barrel roll and leveled off five hundred feet closer to the grassland.

Grimaldi pulled up the nose as soon as he had his pitch level. He looked down but none of his instruments were working. He found himself flying with the technological input available to a 1920s barnstormer, in a shot-to-hell plane in the middle of a storm.

Grimaldi had to fight to keep from screaming in frustration.

He looked down at the floor of the cockpit. He laughed, an edge of hysteria audible. Bolan's leg jerked, and as Grimaldi's gaze ran up the big man's body he saw the chest heaving as Bolan struggled to breathe. Color rushed back into the wounded man's face and his eyes, still dull and glassy, moved and blinked. Bolan was far from out of the woods. Grimaldi still had to get to the DEA field base in Ghana where an emergency medical team, comprised of Navy medics assigned to the Marines at the U.S. Embassy, had been assembled.

Hal Brognola had gone to Justice, Justice had gone to State and State had arranged it with the Interior Minister of Ghana in a telephone game of hot potato.

"We'll make it, Sarge, I promise," Grimaldi said.

"I know," the Executioner whispered.

It was two days before the rain finally broke again. By the time the CIA officer in the DEA field station at Wa, Ghana, launched the RQ-1 UAV Predator drone, Bolan was on a Navy hospital ship in the Atlantic Ocean.

The Predator dropped its Hellfire missile payload straight into the structure at programmed GPS coordinates. The first warhead, designed to penetrate reactive armor on military vehicles, detonated on contact with the front door of the building once used by former Iraqi dictator Saddam Hussein.

The second warhead in the assembly entered the building interior and detonated in-target, vaporizing internal support structures and causing an immediate collapse. A legacy of evil was purged by white-hot cleansing fire.

The drone operator radioed his supervisors in the U.S.

Embassy and reported his success. His superiors in turn alerted the officials seated next to Hal Brognola. By the time Brognola told Barbara Price she'd already heard it from Aaron Kurtzman.

No one outside of Stony Man operations would ever know of the sacrifice and pain getting those coordinates had caused. It would never appear on the front page of the *New York Times* or serve as conversational fodder for the talking heads on cable news channels.

The Executioner's private war would continue.